"You don't have to help me clear my name if you don't want to," Deacon said.

"A bet's a bet," Liberty answered.

"And I'll help you, too. With Mercer and your mother."

"Seriously?" That cheered her.

"It's my job to make my client happy if I can, and reconciling with your mom will make Mercer happy."

"Thank you, thank you!" Without thinking, she laid her cheek on his chest and hugged him hard.

It was wonderful. Deacon, all rock-hard muscles and impressive height, made her feel soft and small and utterly feminine. He hugged her back, too, pressing his lips to the top of her head.

Friendly, chaste and as far as things should probably go. Liberty didn't know much about attorney ethics. Kissing her surely violated one or two of them. Even if she wanted a kiss more than anything.

She should stop this hug now. For Deacon's sake. But when she tried to pull away, he held her fast.

"Not yet," he said, his voice suddenly husky as he dipped his head.

Dear Reader,

Welcome to Reckless, Arizona!

I just love saying those words—or ones like them—because it means I'm launching a brand-new series and introducing my readers to a whole bunch of new characters. I feel kind of as if I'm taking my child to school for their very first day, or showing up for my first day of work at a new job. It's a little scary and a lot exciting. Will they like me? Will I fit in? Will I do well?

I often talk about where I live, in the foothills of the stunning McDowell Mountains. But there are so many other beautiful, fascinating and even quirky places in Arizona. This time, I chose to set my series in a fictional town near Roosevelt Lake, a stunningly beautiful and, frankly, wild area of the state. For such a place, I needed to create a town that was also a bit wild, then populate it with an interesting and complicated family to match.

This first book about the Becketts is the story of Liberty and Deacon. She's trying to piece together a family that's been broken for years. He's trying to clear his name and find out who really caused a terrible bull-goring accident years ago. The odds are stacked against them and against the attraction they feel for one another. In order for them to prevail and find true love, they're going to have to learn some very hard lessons.

I'm thrilled to bring you their story. And, as always, I love hearing from you.

Warmest wishes,

Cathy McDavid

www.CathyMcDavid.com
www.Facebook.com/CathyMcDavid
www.Twitter.com/CathyMcDavid

MORE THAN
A COWBOY

—

CATHY McDAVID

HARLEQUIN® AMERICAN ROMANCE®

Recycling programs
for this product may
not exist in your area.

ISBN-13: 978-0-373-75529-5

MORE THAN A COWBOY

Copyright © 2014 by Cathy McDavid

All rights reserved. Except for use in any review, the reproduction or
utilization of this work in whole or in part in any form by any electronic,
mechanical or other means, now known or hereinafter invented, including
xerography, photocopying and recording, or in any information storage
or retrieval system, is forbidden without the written permission of the
publisher, Harlequin Enterprises Limited, 225 Duncan Mill Road,
Don Mills, Ontario M3B 3K9, Canada.

This is a work of fiction. Names, characters, places and incidents are
either the product of the author's imagination or are used fictitiously,
and any resemblance to actual persons, living or dead, business
establishments, events or locales is entirely coincidental.

This edition published by arrangement with Harlequin Books S.A.

For questions and comments about the quality of this book,
please contact us at CustomerService@Harlequin.com.

® and TM are trademarks of Harlequin Enterprises Limited or its
corporate affiliates. Trademarks indicated with ® are registered in the
United States Patent and Trademark Office, the Canadian Intellectual
Property Office and in other countries.

Printed in U.S.A.

ABOUT THE AUTHOR

For the past eighteen years Cathy McDavid has been juggling a family, a job and writing, and doing pretty well at it, except for the housecleaning part. "Mostly" retired from the corporate business world, she writes full-time from her home in Scottsdale, Arizona, near the breathtaking McDowell Mountains. Her twins have "mostly" left home, returning every now and then to raid her refrigerators. On weekends, she heads to her cabin in the mountains, always taking her laptop with her. You can visit her website at www.cathymcdavid.com.

Books by Cathy McDavid

HARLEQUIN AMERICAN ROMANCE

*Mustang Valley
†Sweetheart, Nevada

To all the cowboys, past and present.
You are true American heroes.

Chapter One

He wasn't here.

No surprise, really, thought Liberty Beckett. She'd arrived—a glance at the clock on the wall behind the long counter confirmed it—fifteen minutes early.

Relief battled with worry for control of her emotions. Was he still coming? Had he changed his mind? A deep breath failed to quell the tension that had been her constant companion this past week.

"You want a table or a booth, honey?"

Liberty blinked. A plump waitress had appeared from nowhere, cradling a stack of oversize plastic menus in the crook of her arm.

"Um, I'm not sure." She took stock of the restaurant that was as familiar to her as the local market or corner gas station. She must have eaten here two, no, three hundred times. The lunch crowd had long departed, and the dinner crowd wasn't due for another hour. A lone customer sat at the counter, nursing a cup of coffee.

Really? In this heat?

Liberty wiped her damp forehead. "I think I'll wait until my…" Her what? Father? Technically, yes. "Until my, um, other party arrives."

"Sure thing." The waitress, someone Liberty knew by

sight after all her years of patronage, gave her a funny look before bustling off.

Other party? Where had that come from?

Liberty silently chided herself and took a seat on the bench just inside the restaurant's front door. Better to wait for Mercer here than at a table or a booth. No awkward pushing out of her seat, going for a hug when he only wanted to shake her hand.

Mercer. *Her father.* Not just the man who was father to Liberty's half sister and brother. No, make that full sister and full brother. Her mother had lied. Since the day Liberty was born. Probably from the day she was conceived. For twenty-four years.

How could she?

Why did she?

Liberty had sacrificed a lot of sleep recently, tossing that question around and around in her head. At one time, she might have understood her mother's motives for keeping such a huge secret. But her *father*—the word still sounded strange to her—had been sober for longer than Liberty could remember. At least, according to her brother's infrequent communications. Several times a year their mother called Ryder, usually on birthdays or holidays. He never called them.

The rift that had developed between her parents before Liberty was born had only widened through the decades, becoming impossible to repair after Ryder left to live with their father. Could that really be twenty-two years ago? Liberty, a toddler at the time, didn't remember Ryder ever living with them. It had always been just her, her sister, Cassidy, and their mother for so very long.

Three women running the Easy Money Rodeo Arena. Probably no one had thought they'd succeed in a predominantly man's world. But they'd proved the skeptics wrong. How different Liberty's life might have been if she'd known Mercer Beckett was her father and not some I-can't-remember-his-name cowboy passing through, as her mother always claimed.

Why had she lied? Liberty kept coming back to the same question. Maybe Mercer could provide the answer, if she worked up the courage to ask him.

The door to the restaurant swung open, and Liberty swore her heart exploded inside her chest. She turned at the same instant a wave of adrenaline swept through her.

Not him! She hugged her middle and tried to collect her wildly scattered wits.

"Morning, Liberty. Is this seat taken?"

Looking up into the tanned, handsome face of Deacon McCrea, she murmured, "N-no," and automatically scooted to her left, making room for him. "Go right ahead."

He smiled as he sat, his brown eyes crinkling attractively at the corners. "I promise not to crowd you."

Only he did. His large frame consumed over half the available space on the bench. Their elbows inadvertently brushed.

"Sorry," he said.

"No worries." Liberty shifted her purse to her other side.

There was only one bench in the Flat Iron Restaurant. She didn't dare suggest Deacon wait outside. He'd melt. A hundred degrees in the shade was typical for summers in Reckless, Arizona. Today's temperatures exceeded that.

Besides, she and Deacon were friends. In a manner of speaking. Acquaintances for sure. He boarded his two horses at the Easy Money and, since his recent return, regularly entered the arena's team penning competitions.

She'd seen him around a lot, at the arena and in town, and that was okay with her. More than once, she'd intentionally put herself in his path, hoping he'd get the hint and ask her out. So far, no luck. But she wasn't giving up.

She sensed her interest in him was reciprocated, even if he hadn't acted on it. Yet.

Any other day, their unexpected encounter would be a perfect opportunity for her to flirt and hint at hooking up. Except Liberty was much too anxious about meeting Mercer to relax, much less ply her feminine wiles.

Biting her lower lip, she studied the clock on the wall again. Ten minutes to go.

Deacon removed his cowboy hat and balanced it on his knee, drawing her attention. "Are you meeting someone, too?" she asked, disliking the slight tremor in her voice.

Damn Mercer for making her nervous. Damn her mother for the lies she'd told.

"A client."

He had nice eyes. Dark and fathomless when he was concentrating, sparkling when he laughed. "Ah, business," she said. "I usually see you on horseback and forget you're an attorney."

"Thank you for not calling me a shyster or a shark."

She drew back to stare at him. "Do people really do that?"

"Not to my face, anyway." He chuckled. "I've been called worse."

Einstein. The cruel taunt suddenly came back to Liberty. She'd been in junior high, and Deacon in high school, but she remembered when he'd worked afternoons and weekends at her family's rodeo arena. More than that, she remembered the terrible treatment he'd received at the hands of his peers, all because school hadn't come easy for him.

Obviously, things had changed. Graduating law school and passing the bar required enormous intelligence and dedication.

"I saw a sign for your office on Sage Brush Drive."

He nodded. "I just moved into the space a few weeks ago."

"It's a good area."

Good area? What was she, the local real estate agent? Liberty suppressed a groan. Nerves again. The most banal of comments were issuing from her mouth. Deacon's proximity wasn't helping matters.

She briefly wondered what had happened to him in the eleven years he'd been away from Reckless, besides becoming an attorney. He'd departed under such bad circumstances, shortly after the horrible bull-goring accident. Some said he'd run away, an action that proved his guilt.

Liberty refused to believe for one second he'd allowed the bull to escape and injure that cowboy. Deacon had been the Becketts' most responsible hand. Unfortunately, her mother hadn't seen it that way and, along with others, pointed the finger of blame at him. No wonder he'd left.

The door to the restaurant whooshed open again, causing her to jerk in response. Deacon looked curiously at her but didn't comment. Thank goodness.

A trio of boisterous young men entered on an explosion of laughter. Tourists. Judging from their sunburned faces, they'd spent the day at Roosevelt Lake thirty miles up the highway. Liberty pegged them as water-skiers rather than fishermen. Their slip-on canvas sneakers, wraparound sunglasses and swim trunks covered by baggy T-shirts gave them away.

Outdoor enthusiasts made up only a small portion of the visitors to Reckless, and they mostly happened to stop on their way to and from Phoenix. The rest were cowfolk. The Easy Money Rodeo Arena and its four annual PCA rodeos made Reckless a regular stop on the circuit for competitors from all over North America.

A colorful and lawless history only added to the appeal. The town's first citizens were, in fact, a notorious gang of outlaws known for their "reckless" escapades. They hadn't settled in the area as much as hidden out in the nearby hills.

Once, Mercer had been a large part of the Easy Money, running it with Liberty's mother, and an active member of the community. Then, he'd started drinking.

Would he be welcomed back? Certainly not by her mother. Liberty had yet to say anything about the meeting to anyone, choosing instead to wait and see how it went.

She forced herself not to check the clock a third time and focused on Deacon. "Have you been getting a lot of new clients?" All right, the question wasn't quite as banal as the others.

"Some. Reckless is still a small town."

"True. But we have no attorneys. The closest ones are in Globe." Almost an hour away. Liberty should know. She'd made more than one trip there to deliver various legal documents to the Becketts' attorney.

"I'm hoping to corner the market."

He had a dry sense of humor. That was new. Deacon had been painfully shy as a teenager, no doubt the result of being constantly picked on by his peers. She'd felt sorry for him. Not only did he have difficulty with school, his home life was a mess. The kind of mess people in a small town loved to gossip about.

As a result, he'd pulled at her teenage heartstrings. Now he pulled at her heart for an entirely different reason.

What did he think of the grown-up her? Oh, if only she weren't in such a state about meeting Mercer, she'd find out.

"I'm sure you'll do well." An idea suddenly occurred to her. "Hey, maybe I could talk to my mom about hiring you. Our liability agreement is probably really outdated."

His features instantly clouded. "I appreciate it, but I have to say no. Conflict of interest."

"Because we already have an attorney?"

"I'm sorry, I can't discuss it." He appeared genuinely distressed.

Though there was no real reason, Liberty felt hurt. She'd

been sure their attraction these past two months since his return was mutual.

Wait! That must be it. He didn't want to take on the Becketts as clients because then he couldn't ask her out.

She said nothing more. Just sat and smiled to herself, her fingers twisting the jade ring on her right hand. She had a whole new reason to be nervous.

The sudden sound of the front door opening had her jumping up from her seat. It was him. Mercer! She recognized him from the pictures she'd researched on the internet.

Their glances connected, and her knees turned to butter.

"Liberty?" Removing his cowboy hat, Mercer combed his fingers through his too long gray hair.

Beside her, Deacon also stood. If not for his hand on her elbow, she might have wobbled ungracefully. Fortunately, he just as quickly released her...and went nowhere.

Oh, this was awkward. For several lengthy seconds, they all three stared at one another.

"You're so pretty." Mercer's gaze took her in from head to toe as if she were a newly minted marvel. "Just like your mother."

Liberty swallowed, surprised to find a lump the size of a golf ball lodged in her throat. She did look like Sunny Beckett and nothing at all like her brother and sister, which was probably why she'd never directly questioned the lies her mother told.

But behind Sunny's back? That was an altogether different thing. The frequent tales she'd heard from the townsfolk about Mercer and her mother, with their many conflicting versions, was why Liberty had begun to dig into her parentage.

Her father hadn't been hard to find. She'd started searching a few months ago after a conversation with Ricky, her team penning partner. The subject of Mercer came up—

it often did even after all these years. Ricky had told her about Mercer being at the Wild West Days Rodeo twenty-five years ago. He'd been adamant and claimed to have a photo somewhere. Liberty's mother always swore Mercer had left before the rodeo. Liberty couldn't forget the conversation and began poking around. Those who could remember confirmed Ricky's story.

It had required all of Liberty's courage to contact Mercer. He'd been nice and readily taken her call. Turned out, he'd had his own suspicions about being her father. The DNA test was simple enough to conduct. Once the results were in, they'd made their plans.

And now he stood before her, his arms open. She went into them with only the slightest hesitation.

He smelled like aftershave. Liberty inhaled deeply, committing the scent to memory.

Mercer hugged her warmly. "There, there, girl."

Only when he'd murmured the endearment did she notice she was crying. Wiping at her cheeks, she straightened and reluctantly withdrew. So that was what it felt like to be held in a father's embrace.

"Do you want to sit?" she asked, her voice quavering.

"Sure thing." A grin spread across his whiskered face.

For an instant, Liberty saw her brother, Ryder. Or, what Ryder would look like if he ever grinned. She couldn't recall seeing him happy. Maybe learning they shared the same father would change that. Maybe he'd come home, too.

Scanning the restaurant, she spotted the waitress heading toward the counter and motioned that she and Mercer would be taking a nearby booth.

"Come on." She led the way…only to pull up short after three steps and peer over her shoulder.

Deacon was following them. She'd forgotten all about him.

"Is there, um, something you want?"

He addressed Mercer rather than her. "Would you like me to wait here?"

"No." Mercer clasped Deacon's shoulder. "Join us."

"W-why?" Liberty stared at the two of them in confusion.

"Deacon is my attorney," Mercer said.

"Your attorney?"

"I'll explain." He took over, directing them to a table rather than a booth.

Liberty followed him, her confusion mounting. Why did Mercer need legal counsel? And why bring his counsel to their meeting?

"What's going on? Tell me," she insisted the moment they were seated, Mercer to her left and Deacon across from her. Was that intentional? In the wide-open restaurant, she felt cornered.

"Liberty," Mercer began slowly, "I'm so glad you contacted me. Learning you're my daughter, well, it's just about the best news I've ever had." He paused, appearing to choose his words carefully. "The thing is, your mother and I have a complicated history. And a long-standing business arrangement."

"Business arrangement?"

"I own half of the Easy Money. Not only that, your mother owes me a considerable amount of money. I'm here to meet you and to get to know you. But I'm also here to collect what is rightfully mine. Deacon has agreed to represent me. While I don't want to bring a lawsuit against your mother…"

Liberty had trouble understanding the rest of what Mercer said. It was hard to hear him above the roar of her world crashing down around her.

DEACON WATCHED LIBERTY'S BACK as she all but bolted from the restaurant, his gut twisting into a tight knot. The meeting went exactly as he'd expected it would: not well.

He'd told Mercer when they met at his office yesterday that springing his true intentions on Liberty right from the get-go wasn't the best move. Mercer had been adamant. He and Liberty had both been denied the truth for years. He refused to start out his relationship with her by following in her mother's footsteps.

Deacon understood. He also felt sorry for Liberty. She must be reeling. He'd go after her if he could and…do what? Tell her he wished things were different? That he'd been taken by her from the moment they met again his third day back and wanted to ask her out, only he hadn't found the courage? Too late now. Mercer was his client and dating his daughter was out of the question.

Instead, he suggested, "Should you check on her?"

Mercer considered before answering. "Might be better to give her some time. If she's as much her mother's daughter as I suspect, she's not ready to listen."

Deacon decided to let Mercer be the judge. Through the large window, he watched Liberty's SUV leave the parking lot and considered stopping by the Easy Money later.

Their waitress sidled up to the table and distributed menus. "Will the young lady be returning?"

"I don't think so." Mercer's tone was noncommittal.

"Can I start you off with something to drink?"

"You still have that fresh-squeezed lemonade?"

"Got a fresh pitcher in the cooler."

"I'll take a large glass." Mercer beamed at the woman. For someone who had just devastated his long-lost daughter with upsetting news, he didn't look particularly distressed.

Or was he? People often put on a show to hide their true feelings. Deacon knew that better than most. He was putting on a show right now.

"And for you?" the waitress prompted.

"Iced tea." After the past few minutes, Deacon could really use something stronger.

He'd always liked Liberty, though she'd been barely more than a kid when he worked at the arena. He himself had been a skinny, awkward high school senior. She was kind to him when others weren't. More than that, she'd defended him after the accident involving the bulls. Her mother and older sister, Cassidy, on the other hand, had only accusations for him. False ones.

Mercer waited until their waitress had left to resume their conversation. "She'll go straight to Sunny, naturally."

"You sound like you're counting on it."

He chuckled, more to himself than out loud.

Deacon didn't bother perusing the menu. He'd lost his appetite. Instead, he powered up his tablet. "It might have been better for us to approach your ex-wife first."

"I don't think it'll make a difference. Sunny knew I'd return eventually."

The sum she owed Mercer was indeed considerable. Six figures. Most people wouldn't have waited all those years to collect. Deacon considered his client's motives. Would Mercer have returned to Reckless if Liberty hadn't contacted him out of the blue, suggesting he might be her biological father?

Somehow, Deacon didn't think so. Mercer definitely had an agenda. Deacon couldn't fault the man. He himself had a private agenda and Mercer retaining him as his attorney fit perfectly into his plans.

It was why, as much as he liked Liberty and was attracted to her, he chose to take on Mercer as a client over any potential relationship with her. He hoped he didn't regret his decision.

"Have you had a chance yet to draw up the demand

letter?" Mercer inquired after their beverages arrived and the waitress took his dinner order.

Deacon scrolled through a document on his tablet. "I'm still reviewing the terms of your property settlement with Sunny. The language is a little ambiguous in some places."

"It was written a long time ago."

"Did you ever attempt to collect your share of the arena revenues?"

"Nah." He dismissed Deacon's question with a frown. "Didn't need it. I've done just fine for myself."

Deacon guessed the older man was probably comfortable. Experienced bucking stock foremen earned decent wages, and Mercer Beckett was considered to be one of the best. It stood to reason. Decades earlier, he'd been one of the best bull riders in the country.

Why then the sudden interest in seeking his share of the revenues? It wasn't greed or financial need. And how did Liberty figure into it? Deacon's natural curiosity was piqued.

"I'll have a draft of the demand letter done first thing in the morning."

"Good." Mercer nodded approvingly. "I'd like for us to visit the Easy Money as soon as possible with the letter in hand. What time can I come by your office in the morning?"

"Nine. Be prepared, Mrs. Beckett's attorney will most likely request changes."

"Such as?"

"An extension. It's what I'd recommend if I were her counsel."

"I won't give it tō her."

"You might rethink that," Deacon said. "She doesn't have that kind of money. I've already checked into her finances."

Mercer and Sunny's divorce agreement was atypical, to

say the least. In exchange for paying no child support, Mercer let Sunny keep all the revenue from the Easy Money Rodeo Arena, an amount far exceeding any child support he would have been required to pay. Even after his son, Ryder, came to live with him two years after the divorce, and later when their daughter Cassidy turned eighteen and Mercer was entitled to the money, he didn't take a single cent.

Some might say his were the actions of a decent guy. Except now Mercer was coming after Sunny for all the back and possibly future payments. It was a puzzling contradiction.

"I want her to feel like she has no choice."

Deacon decided to be blunt. "Can I ask why?"

The older man winked. "So she'll take the partnership agreement we're going to offer her instead."

"Partnership agreement?"

This was the first Mercer had mentioned any such thing. Deacon should have seen it coming.

"I'm going to be a part of my daughters' lives. Sunny won't allow it unless she has no choice. The arena and the money she owes me are my way in." His eyes softened, crinkling at the corners. "She's stubborn. And willful."

Deacon was hardly a romantic, so his sudden revelation came as a bit of a shock. "You still love her."

"Never stopped."

"You want her back."

"Always have. But there wasn't a snowball's chance in hell until now."

"Mercer, I'm not sure a forced partnership and using Liberty is the right course of action for winning over your ex-wife. If she's as stubborn and willful as you say—"

"She'll come around. Sooner or later. Until then, co-managing the arena will give me a reason to see her every day and get to know my daughters."

"Good luck with that." From what Deacon knew of Sunny Beckett, Mercer had his work cut out for him.

Mercer's meal arrived. While he ate and Deacon finished a refill of his iced tea, they discussed the terms of the partnership agreement.

"We need to see copies of the arena's financial statements before finalizing any agreement," Deacon said. "The last five years at least."

"Sunny will have them. She's a whiz when it comes to the books and money. It's one of the reasons we were able to build the arena up from practically nothing."

Deacon maintained a neutral expression. Mercer's drinking almost drove the arena into the ground. Sunny was clearly one sharp businesswoman. She'd built up the arena from practically nothing—twice.

"First order of business," Mercer eagerly announced, "is to increase the bucking stock operation. Sunny has let most of it go since the accident."

Mercer knew about the accident with the bull and that the blame had been pinned on Deacon. He'd told Deacon in their meeting yesterday that he didn't care about a youthful mistake. Plenty of more experienced bucking stock handlers made worse mistakes than that.

When Deacon insisted on his innocence, Mercer's response had been simply, "All the better."

"You can't purchase new bucking stock without her consent," Deacon said.

"What if I use my own money?"

"She'll still have to consent. That's how most partnership agreements are worded."

"Change the wording."

Deacon typed another note into his tablet. "Her attorney will fight it."

"Don't know until we try."

Before, Deacon would have seen Mercer's confidence

as cocky and arrogant. Now, he knew the reason behind it. The man was in love and, evidently, eternally optimistic.

He sure did have a funny way of demonstrating that love.

Not that Deacon was suave and sophisticated when it came to ladies. His acute reading disability hadn't just held him back in school. Even when he'd learned to compensate, old habits were hard to break.

Take Liberty, for example. He'd had multiple opportunities to pursue her but hadn't acted on them. Like Mercer said, she was pretty, with her short blond hair that didn't look anything like a cowgirl's. Neither did all those rings she wore, which he hadn't noticed before today.

The boots and jeans were another story. He couldn't take his eyes off her incredibly long legs when she was riding. It had cost him more than one disqualification when they were team penning together.

"Can you call Sunny and tell her to expect us tomorrow? After lunch sometime." Mercer sopped up the last bit of chicken gravy with a chunk of dinner roll.

"No problem."

"And ask her to make sure Cassidy and Liberty are there, too. This concerns all three of them."

Deacon exhaled. He should have known Liberty would be there.

Despite his interest in her and the thoughts he couldn't get out of his head no matter what, he hadn't hesitated when Mercer approached him seeking representation. Having access to the arena's records was exactly what Deacon needed to aid his own cause. For that, he would sacrifice a great deal.

Someone other than Deacon had left the bull's gate unlatched that terrible day, and he intended to find out who. Then, armed with proof positive, he'd see to it Sunny Beckett and everyone else in Reckless knew the truth. Deacon would live in shame no more.

Chapter Two

"How could you?"

"Come on. Give Mom a break."

Liberty sighed expansively and slumped down into the kitchen chair. For the past half hour, her sister, Cassidy, had been defending their mother while Liberty had paced back and forth in front of the sink, venting her outrage at being lied to and her anger at the turn of events. If she'd been told the truth from the beginning, none of this would have happened.

A lawsuit! And that was only a small portion of what Liberty was grappling with. The father she'd known for an entire five minutes had used her in his scheme to get the money owed him. Money!

Did he realize that, as employees of the arena, Liberty and Cassidy would be profoundly affected?

The scent of Mercer's aftershave filled the air. Or maybe it was no more than a memory. One she'd be better off without. Refocusing her attention, she looked at her mother sitting across the table—and saw a stranger.

"What else haven't you told us, Mom?" she asked.

"Nothing." The response was uttered through tight lips. She'd been angry since being confronted.

"Yeah." Liberty snorted derisively. "I guess the identity

of my real father, his half ownership in our rodeo arena and the money you owe him are enough."

"That's not fair! I did what I thought was best to protect you."

"From what? A reformed alcoholic who hadn't touched a drop in twenty-two years? A man who, by all accounts, was a good father to his son?"

During most of their long, emotionally draining exchange, Sunny had sat at the table, enough sparks flashing in her eyes to ignite a brush fire.

"I don't trust him," she blurted out. "And with good reason."

"Maybe once. Not for years. You had no right to screw with my life."

"That's enough." Sunny slapped the table with her hand.

Liberty fumed. What did her mother have to be so mad about? Mercer's return? She had to assume he'd approach her for the money one day. The amount was a staggering sum. Over one hundred thousand dollars. When Sunny informed them, Liberty had physically gulped. Their savings didn't cover a fourth of that.

Cassidy, too, though she'd regained her composure quickly, making up for their mother's silence with more verbal attacks on Mercer.

"She was thinking of us," Cassidy said, her tone superior. "Like a good mother does."

Younger by eleven years, Liberty had always been the baby of the family, doted on by her mother and ruled over by her big sister. Liberty might be twenty-four, but as far as Cassidy was concerned, their relationship hadn't changed.

"Please." Liberty leaned forward and waited for her mother to meet her gaze. A sudden surge of emotion tightened her voice. "I need to know. Why did you lie to me?"

The topic of Mercer and the money owed him had been

temporarily set aside. Liberty instead pressed for the information most important to her.

"Trust me," Cassidy quipped. "You don't want Mercer Beckett for a father. He nearly killed us both."

Killing might be a stretch. On his way home from picking up Cassidy at a friend's house, an inebriated Mercer lost control of the pickup he was driving and slammed into the well house. Thankfully, no one was injured. The same couldn't be said for the well house. But the wreck had terrified Cassidy and prompted Sunny to send Mercer packing a few weeks later.

Liberty might have sent him packing, too. Especially when he didn't stop drinking immediately afterward. "He must regret what happened," she said to Cassidy.

"If he does, he sure as heck never told me."

Liberty's sister always sided with their mother when it came to Mercer. With good cause, Liberty supposed. As far as Cassidy was concerned, Mercer's past sins were unforgivable. Whereas Sunny hardly ever mentioned him, Cassidy seized every opportunity to speak ill. Daddy's little girl hadn't ever gotten over her hurt and resentment at his going from perfect father to raging alcoholic. Also fear. His drinking and actions while under the influence had scared her.

From what Liberty was able to determine, both her siblings had once adored their father. Ryder's devotion, however, hadn't ever wavered despite Mercer's drinking problem. At fourteen, when he could legally choose which parent to reside with, he left Reckless and joined Mercer in Kingman, a town nearly a full day's drive away.

Cassidy's adoration of Mercer had soured. Liberty suspected their mother's refusal to discuss him only hardened the shell surrounding her sister's heart.

"Twenty-two years of sobriety is more than enough to prove he's changed," Liberty insisted. "I had the right to make my own decision regarding Mercer. Ryder did."

Sunny jerked involuntarily at the mention of her estranged son. Then, to Liberty's shock, her mother burst into tears.

Her fury instantly waned. It must have been heartbreaking for her mother to lose Ryder. And all her attempts to maintain contact with him had either been ignored or thrown back in her face. He resented their mother as much as Cassidy did their father—and Liberty was caught in the middle.

The stranger Liberty saw across the table disappeared, and her mother once more sat there.

"I'm sorry," she said. "I know you miss Ryder and wish things were different. But that doesn't change the fact you should have told me about Mercer being my father."

"I wanted to." Sunny wiped her tears with a paper napkin from the holder on the table. "You have no idea how many times I tried."

"What stopped you?"

"I lost my courage. I was so afraid you'd go looking for him."

Like Ryder. The truth at last. Liberty supposed she understood her mother's fear. Losing one child had been difficult enough.

"You think we would have had it so good if he'd been draining our bank account dry every month?" Cassidy interjected.

For the first time, Sunny defended Mercer. "It wasn't like that. He couldn't have drained us dry. There were clauses in our property settlement agreement. The monthly profits had to be at a certain level or the full amount he was owed went back into the operating account to insure sufficient cash flow."

"In other words—" Liberty sent her sister a pointed look "—he cared about the arena and us and made sure we wouldn't hit rock bottom again."

Cassidy huffed and leaned against the counter, her arms crossed. "Before you go awarding him a big shiny halo, just remember he wants the money now."

"He'll take payments."

"You don't know that."

"He won't have a choice."

"Girls!"

At their mother's sharp outburst, both Liberty and Cassidy shut their mouths.

"Why didn't you put the money aside?" Liberty asked a moment later when she and her sister were both calmer. "Just in case he came to collect."

"I did at first." Sunny was also calmer. "A couple hundred dollars a week. But Cassidy was competing on the rodeo circuit in those days. She needed money for a horse and training and a new saddle. With her gone so much, I was shorthanded and had to hire part-time help."

Barrel racing was the same as any other rodeo event. Decent winnings could be had at the championship level. Getting there, however, required money, and Sunny had footed the bill.

Did Cassidy ever repay their mother? Liberty considered asking but held her tongue. In Cassidy's current mood, she wouldn't appreciate the underlying accusation.

"Then there was the accident and poor Ernie Tuckerman." Sunny wrung her hands together. "I had a ten-thousand-dollar deductible to cover, and afterward, our insurance premiums skyrocketed. It was six years since Cassidy's high school graduation. I figured if Mercer hadn't demanded his share of the revenue by then, he wasn't ever going to."

A peculiar arrangement, Liberty thought, not for the first time since hearing about it. Mercer hadn't paid any child support for Cassidy. Instead, he'd let their mother keep all the arena profits until Cassidy graduated high school. At that point, her mother was supposed to start paying him his share. Only she hadn't. And he didn't ask for it.

Sunny had obviously said nothing about his half ownership of the arena to Cassidy, either. Liberty had seen the shock and disbelief on her sister's face when she'd blurted the news. Yet, Cassidy had blamed Mercer rather than their mother.

"You and Mercer must have talked over the years," Liberty said. "Did he ever mention the money?"

Sunny shook her head. "The few times we did talk, the subject of money didn't come up. That's the truth," she reiterated.

There was a wistfulness in her mother's expression that Liberty had seen before. When she was young, she'd caught her mother studying a framed photograph, that same expression on her face. Later, Liberty had snuck into her mother's room and removed the photo from its hiding place in the back of the drawer. A younger version of her parents stared back at her, except Liberty hadn't known Mercer was her father.

When she'd asked about Mercer, her mother changed the subject. Eventually, Liberty stopped asking—but not wondering.

"Did he ever talk about me?" Her tongue tripped over the last word.

"To ask if you were his?"

Liberty nodded, not trusting herself to speak. Mercer must have realized she'd been born nine months, give or take, after he and her mother split.

"He did."

"You lied to him, too!"

"He was drinking then. Heavily. I didn't want to give him any reason to stick around."

Emotions rose up in Liberty, threatening to choke her.

She fought for control. "He must have been so hurt. Thinking you slept with another man within days after he left."

Sunny remained mute, her features dark.

"He hurt us!" Cassidy insisted. Tears had welled in the corners of her eyes.

Liberty shot to her feet, the need to distance herself for a moment overpowering her. Sunny had lied to Mercer and driven him away rather than let him know he'd fathered a third child with her.

"Tell me this, Mom." She hesitated on her way to the door. The barn, with its familiar scent of horses and dark, cool corners, beckoned. It had been her sanctuary since she was a little girl, the place she went to when she wanted to be alone. "If you despised Mercer so much, why did you sleep with him right up to the day you threw him out?"

If she meant to wound her mother, she succeeded. Sunny's control collapsed, and her features crumpled.

Liberty wasn't quite to the door when the arena phone rang. Extensions had been placed in the kitchen and Sunny's bedroom in case of emergencies. With no one manning the office, they'd been answering the phone in the house.

Being the closest, Liberty grabbed the receiver, put it to her ear and automatically said, "Easy Money Rodeo Arena, Liberty Beckett speaking."

"Hello, Liberty. It's Deacon McCrea."

She went still, and despite her resolve to the contrary, her insides fluttered as they often did when she spoke to him. Dammit. After the meeting with Mercer, he was off-limits. Apparently, her heart hadn't gotten the memo yet.

"Hello," he said. "Did I lose you?"

"N-no." She turned toward her mother and sister. They'd been as unnerved as her to learn Deacon McCrea was representing Mercer. The irony wasn't lost on Liberty. They'd blamed him for the bull-goring accident regardless of any evidence. "What do you want, Deacon?"

The alarm on their faces matched the panic Liberty felt.

"Is your mother available?" he asked.

She held the phone away and pressed the mute button. "He wants to talk to you."

Sunny shook her head vehemently.

Liberty returned to the call. "I'm sorry. She's not in at the moment."

"Could you give her a message for me?"

"What is it?"

Liberty hadn't intended to sound so curt with Deacon. Nothing about this situation with her family was his fault. But he'd positioned himself squarely in Mercer's camp and had to know that squashed any potential relationship with her. She did, and grieved just a little for what was lost.

"Your father and I would like to meet with you, your mother and sister tomorrow. Is one o'clock convenient?"

"For what?"

"To discuss terms. Can Sunny or someone else call me back and confirm? Here's my number."

Discuss terms? An ambiguous phrase that held the power to tear their lives apart.

With shaking fingers, Liberty reached for the pad and pen kept by the phone and jotted down the number he recited.

"I'm not sure we're available," she said. "It's summer. I teach riding classes both mornings and afternoons, and my mother—"

"The sooner the better."

His abrupt businesslike manner caused her to bristle. To think she'd wasted all those hours daydreaming about him, now *and* in the past.

"Fine. I'll give her the message." Hanging up, she faced

her family. "Mercer has requested a meeting. It doesn't sound like he'll take no for an answer."

DEACON PULLED INTO the Easy Money Rodeo Arena grounds and was instantly transported eleven years into the past. That hadn't happened for weeks. Lately, he'd begun to hope the past was dead, that he might actually belong here again and have a chance with Liberty. Turned out he'd been wrong. On all three counts. He wasn't sure which disappointed him the most.

Relocating to Reckless had been a six-month impulse. He'd returned briefly to handle some old business for his parents. They'd moved to Globe years ago. Several people had recognized Deacon and stopped him on the streets, mentioning the accident. When he left, he vowed never to set eyes on the place again. Except he couldn't get those encounters and the town out of his mind.

He was innocent. He would clear his name. He would not run away again.

Mercer must be going through a similar trip down memory lane for he'd grown suddenly quiet after having talked Deacon's ear off during the entire drive from town.

Maneuvering his pickup into an empty space outside the arena office, Deacon parked and shut off the engine. He reached for the door handle. "You ready?"

Mercer didn't move.

Deacon waited while the cab quickly heated to an uncomfortable temperature.

"Anytime," he prodded.

"Yeah, sorry." Mercer's smile was weak at best. "Got lost in thought there for a second."

Outside the truck, Deacon paused and surveyed his surroundings, much as he had that first day back. On the surface, little had changed.

The office was housed in the main barn and could be

entered from either the outside or inside of the barn. The arena was to the west and directly across from the main barn. Aluminum bleachers flanked the two long sides of the arena. On the south end were bucking chutes, large ones for the bulls and horses, smaller ones for the calves. Narrow runways connected the chutes to the livestock-holding pens. Above the chutes, and with a bird's-eye view, was the announcer's stand.

A lengthy row of shaded stalls had been built behind the main barn, along with more livestock pens and three connected pastures. About half of the box stalls in the main barn and most of the outdoor stalls were available for lease to the public. Deacon himself rented two stalls for his horses.

He'd long ago given up rodeoing. A couple years ago, at the urging of a buddy, he'd started team penning and discovered he not only had a knack for it, he quite enjoyed it. The horses were a gift to himself when he passed the bar exam.

Liberty also had a love of team penning. It was something they'd shared these past couple of months, often practicing and competing together. He was going to miss that.

Deacon and Mercer strode in the direction of the office. An old wooden picnic table sat to the right of the door, the innumerable scars and gouges indistinguishable from the initials and names carved into it. Three folding lawn chairs were clustered near the picnic table. All empty.

At the office door, Deacon paused and knocked. Most people simply entered. He'd decided to give the three Beckett women a quick heads-up. Turned out they weren't there. Instead, the tiny waiting area was deserted, and a woman Deacon didn't immediately recognize occupied the desk.

"Hi." Her smile was guarded. "I'll let Sunny know you're here." She reached for the desk phone and pressed a series of buttons on the dial pad. "Sunny Beckett to the office. Sunny Beckett to the office." Half a beat behind, the receptionist's voice blared from speakers inside the barn and at the arena. "She shouldn't be long," the woman said after hanging up.

"Thank you kindly." Mercer took a seat in one of the two well-worn visitor chairs.

Deacon joined him. He understood this was a game. Sunny didn't want to appear as if she was waiting for them. That would show weakness. Forcing them to wait for her, on her home turf at that, showed strength.

He perused the pictures on the walls. Some were of familiar scenes and faces, others evidently taken after his time here as a wrangler. The ones of the bulls had been removed.

"I remember you," Mercer said. "You're Cassidy's friend."

Deacon swiveled in his chair. Mercer was staring at the woman, the beginnings of a grin on his face.

"Yes," she answered hesitantly.

He snapped his fingers as if a thought had just occurred to him. "Tatum Hanks."

"It's Tatum Mayweather now." Her smile lost some of its wariness. "How are you, Mr. Beckett?"

"Just dandy. And call me Mercer. I take it you work here."

"For the last four months. Before that, I taught third grade at the elementary school."

Deacon watched the woman as she and Mercer chatted. He'd seen her off and on, naturally, and noticed her staring at him, as did anyone who'd been around at the time of the accident. He'd ignored her stares. In hindsight, he should have paid more attention.

She was, he now recalled, Cassidy's friend. Best friend. The few memories he could muster crystalized. One centered on a wedding at the arena.

"How's that husband of yours?" Mercer asked.

Her voice grew quiet. "We're not married anymore."

"Sorry to hear that."

"I have three children." She brightened and turned a framed picture around on her desk for Mercer to see. In between, she cast Deacon hasty glances.

For a moment, he missed the way Liberty looked at him. There was no wariness or accusation in her eyes. Only kindness, humor and undeniable interest.

She wouldn't have that same look today. Her tone during their phone call yesterday had been icy and distant. He anticipated similar treatment at their meeting.

The door leading to the barn opened. Sunny strode inside, accompanied by Cassidy. Neither woman noticed Deacon. They went straight to Mercer, who immediately rose.

"Sunny. Cassidy." He removed his cowboy hat and took them in from head to toe. "Damn, it's good to see you."

They didn't return his enthusiasm. Anything but. And no hugs were initiated.

"You look great. Both of you." He'd included his daughter, but his attention never wavered from Sunny.

Deacon had to admit time had been her friend. A short-sleeved Western-cut shirt tucked into her jeans revealed a still trim and shapely figure. Blond hair a couple shades darker than Liberty's was pulled up into an efficient ponytail. Her green eyes observed Mercer carefully.

Green. Hmm. Liberty's eyes were blue, a deep shade Deacon could easily get lost in.

He mentally shook himself. This meeting was too important for him to abandon focus.

"Let's go into Mom's office." Cassidy started for the connecting door. If she was feeling sentimental, she hid it well.

Deacon had barely stood when Liberty entered. An all-too-common jolt coursed through him. It intensified when their gazes locked.

She was hurt. He could see it in her face. There was no way to change that. No going back. Deacon had made his choice, though not without regrets. He hoped one day she'd understand.

"Liberty!" Mercer beamed. "How are you?"

Give the man credit. He acted as if their visit today was strictly social and nothing out of the ordinary.

She didn't answer him and instead followed her mother and sister into Sunny's office. They were presenting a united front. Even so, Deacon noted a slight underlying tension between the women. He imagined Liberty had posed a lot of questions to her mother yesterday. Perhaps not all had been answered, or answered satisfactorily.

There weren't enough chairs in the office. Sunny sat at her desk, a position of authority. Cassidy dropped into the only available vacant seat. If her intent was to make their visitors suffer discomfort, she didn't succeed.

Undaunted, Mercer said, "Be right back." And he was, with the two chairs from the front office. Carrying one in each arm, he set them down and squeezed them together in front of Sunny's desk.

"My dear." He gestured for Liberty to sit.

She did, and when Mercer plunked down in the middle chair, he and his two daughters were practically rubbing knees. Deacon leaned against a four-drawer file cabinet, which put him directly behind Liberty and looking over her shoulder. She shifted uneasily, then, as if sensing him, turned. The hurt he'd seen earlier was gone, replaced by confusion.

He ignored the pang of guilt—he had to, really—and smiled. "Good afternoon."

Her answer was to face forward.

All right, he deserved that. Tucking the envelope containing the demand letter and draft partnership agreement under his arm, Deacon powered up his tablet and readied to take notes.

"Just so you know, Sunny, I don't want your money."

At Mercer's impromptu announcement, the three women sat suddenly straighter.

"Then why threaten me with a lawsuit?" Sunny asked, her voice ripe with indignation.

"I'd rather manage the Easy Money with you."

Deacon swallowed a groan. Why bother with plans when his client was bound and determined not to stick to them?

Sunny's eyes widened and her jaw went visibly slack.

Cassidy leaped from her chair. "You're crazy!"

Mercer wasn't the least bit put off by her rage. "Just hear me out before you go getting your panties in a twist."

"Who are you to—"

"We all know you don't have the money," he said, cutting Cassidy off.

"I can get it," Sunny interjected.

"How? A loan against the arena? Can't do that without my signature."

"A line of credit at the bank."

"Which would be secured by the arena and also require my consent." Mercer turned to Deacon for confirmation.

"Most likely." Taking his cue, he withdrew the draft partnership agreement from the envelope.

"I own half this arena, Sunny. You can't prevent me from managing it with you. What I'm proposing is that we do it with a mutually acceptable agreement in place rather than as hostile partners."

Deacon almost chuckled at hearing Mercer use the term he'd coined earlier that morning in his office.

"What are the terms of this agreement?" Sunny asked cautiously.

"Mom! You can't be serious." Cassidy glared at Mercer.

"I haven't said yes."

Deacon gave Sunny credit. She was indeed a smart businesswoman, exploring her options with a level head.

What did Liberty think? he wondered. The rigid set of her shoulders led him to believe she wasn't exactly tickled about the prospects of her father joining forces with them. But, unlike her sister, she kept her opinion to herself.

Reaching around her, Deacon passed the draft partnership agreement to Sunny. The demand letter remained in the envelope. They wouldn't need it if Sunny consented.

As he withdrew his arm, Liberty turned. They were inches apart. She stiffened but didn't glance away. Neither did he. Not for several seconds. She was so pretty, and those blue eyes...

Deacon went back to leaning against the file cabinet before he did or said something stupid. This, he decided, could turn out to be a long, long afternoon.

Sunny silently skimmed the documents. After a moment, she tapped the papers into a neat rectangle and cleared her throat.

"Can you excuse us for a few minutes? I'd like to talk to Mercer alone."

"M-Mom," Cassidy sputtered. She appeared on the verge of a meltdown.

Liberty, on the other hand, couldn't exit the office fast enough. Deacon had to flatten himself against the file cabinet in order to let her pass. As she did, he noticed her earrings. Gold dangling things that made no sense for a working cowgirl.

Great. Yet another thing to like about her. Liberty flouted conventionality.

"Mercer?" Clearing his throat, he asked, "Would you like me to stay?"

"No need." His client exuded pleasure. This turn of events must be fitting nicely into his plans.

Deacon waited for Cassidy to precede him out of the office. When a last-ditch silent plea didn't sway her mother, she stormed off. Mercer closed the office door behind Deacon.

The reception area was empty. He debated sitting and waiting. His gut told him the meeting between the two cxes was going to take a while. He decided to check on his horses and then maybe walk the arena grounds. Mercer would call Deacon's cell phone if he needed something.

There were easily fifty head of horses in the main barn. Many of them nickered and stretched their necks over their stall door to investigate. It wasn't mealtime but handouts were always a possibility.

Deacon stopped at the stalls housing his horses. Huck, a young bay gelding with, in Deacon's opinion, potential to be the best cutting horse on the property, greeted him with a lusty snort.

"Hey, boy." Deacon patted the horse's long, smooth neck. In the stall beside him, Confetti pawed the ground, demanding her equal share of attention. "Just wait. You're next."

The spotted Appaloosa mare was his first choice for team penning. She had a natural instinct when it came to calves and could turn on a dime.

"Deacon!"

At the sound of his name, he pivoted.

Liberty stood not ten feet away. "Can we talk?"

"Sure." He lowered his hand. "Not about the agreement. That's confidential—"

"Why are you doing this?"

She didn't appear inclined for a stroll, so he remained standing there, the horse nudging his arm in a bid for more attention. "I'm an attorney. Your father came to me seeking representation, and I don't exactly have an abundance of clients."

Because of her mother's treatment of him after the accident. The unspoken words hung in the air.

"Are you out for revenge?" she demanded.

"I wouldn't stoop that low."

"Then why?"

"This isn't personal, Liberty." Only it was.

"You can't deny your resentment toward my family is going to affect your dealings with my father."

"I promise you it won't." If anything, his attraction to her was more likely to impair his judgment. "Like it or not, this is ultimately between your parents. Neither of us will have much to do with the outcome."

"What do you think will happen?"

He'd put his money on Mercer. What he said, however, was, "I can't speculate. But I will tell you this. I don't believe for one minute your father wants to ruin the arena or your mother's finances."

"And you're really not out to get my family?"

"No."

That seemed to satisfy her, and she walked away.

Watching her go, Deacon suffered another, more wrenching pang of guilt.

Revenge didn't motivate him. It was redemption and exoneration. Deacon would prove his innocence in the accident one way or the other, and he wasn't opposed to using his position as Mercer's attorney to accomplish it.

He only hoped Liberty and her family didn't get hurt in the process.

Chapter Three

Liberty pretended not to notice Deacon's approach. Even if she wasn't currently teaching a riding class of four-, five- and six-year-olds, she wouldn't have acknowledged him. Not after the meeting yesterday.

"That's right, Andrea," she called out. "Put your weight in your heels and keep your back straight. Pay attention, Benjy. Look ahead and stop making faces at your neighbor."

She suppressed a groan. Her nephew Benjamin was the self-appointed class clown.

Nephew! Did Mercer know he had a grandson? He must, right? In all the turmoil of the past two days, Liberty hadn't once stopped to consider her sister's young son. Okay, she had. But that was before Mercer threatened her mother with a lawsuit.

She'd naively assumed grandfather and grandson would be introduced over time and with plenty of preparation. Or not. The decision was Cassidy's to make. Liberty had only wanted to meet her father. She hadn't anticipated all hell breaking loose. And so fast.

Deacon knew about Benjamin, had seen him around the arena. He'd probably discussed Benjamin with Mercer. Could that be why he was approaching the arena, his attention fixated on…what?

Liberty's gaze shot to her nephew. Too late now. She

couldn't very well send the boy away. That would only bring attention to him. No choice except to continue with the lesson and act normal.

"Morning, Liberty."

Swell. He was addressing her. She should have moved to the center of the arena where she'd be out of earshot instead of standing along the fence.

She turned her head a mere fraction of an inch. "Deacon."

He was early to the family meeting. Really early. Like, thirty minutes. He was evidently Mr. Prompt when it came to appointments. She'd gotten that much from the restaurant when they both arrived ahead of schedule. But a whole thirty minutes? And did he have to stand near the bleachers where the students' moms and one dad were all seated?

"Nice day," he said nonchalantly, petting one of the ranch dogs that had crawled out from under the bleachers.

"It's hot," she retorted, and returned to her class. "Dee Dee, even reins. That's it." *Breathe,* Liberty reminded herself. *Relax.* "All right now, I want everyone to trot in a circle. Then, on my cue, reverse and go in the other direction. Remember, no kicking your horse. Just a steady pressure with the insides of your calves."

Horse was a loose description. Two of the students rode ponies and another a small mule. All the mounts were dead broke and reliable as rain during the summer monsoon season—which, judging by the clouds accumulating in the northeast sky, might start any minute.

Liberty liked teaching the younger children much better than the older ones. They were sponges, eager to learn and soak up all the knowledge she could impart. As they grew and gained confidence, they sometimes gave Liberty a hard time. Not that she let them get away with it. Rule number one during any lesson, child or adult: the instructor was in charge.

Feeling a tingling on the back of her neck, she rubbed the spot. A few seconds later, the tingling returned. Deacon! He was staring at her again. She'd experienced the same sensation yesterday in her mother's office.

Then, he'd been standing right behind her. In the Flat Iron Restaurant, they'd been sitting side by side. Now, he was tracking her every move. The part of her that was still attuned to their mutual attraction went on high alert.

He looked good. Taller than when he'd worked here as a teenager and broader in the shoulders. He had a way of making jeans and a Western-cut dress shirt look professional. And his hat—a dark tan Resistol—was pulled down just a touch. Enough to lend a bit of edge to his appearance.

She fought the impulses charging through her. Deacon was her father's attorney. He could be short, bald and ugly for all she cared.

Oh, but he wasn't. She sighed and rubbed the back of her neck again.

The end of the lesson couldn't come fast enough. Except, then they'd be having their "family meeting" in the house. Liberty and Cassidy would learn the details of the new partnership agreement between their parents and precisely what role Mercer would have in the operation of the arena.

He was to be a permanent fixture in their lives. Assuming he didn't grow tired of them and leave. Liberty had yet to come to terms with how she felt. She'd wanted to get to know the man who'd fathered her. Not, however, under these circumstances.

The tangle of lies her mother had told was going to affect them all—possibly for years to come. Liberty tried not to judge her mother too harshly. She was having trouble with that. Her mother's attempt to protect her—protect them—had backfired. Their livelihoods could even now be in jeopardy, depending on what Mercer wanted.

She tried to remain optimistic. He might be an alcoholic—a reformed alcoholic and sober for many, many years—but that wasn't the same as a serial killer or a rapist. And he must care about them and the arena. If not, he would have made things difficult for them long before now.

She *should* have been told about him, Liberty thought with renewed frustration. Then, they wouldn't be in this fix. Frankly, she didn't know who to be angrier with—her mother, Mercer or Deacon. All had lied.

All right, maybe not Deacon so much. He hadn't been under any obligation to tell her he'd taken on her father as a client. But he might have prepared her when they were sitting together in the Flat Iron, their knees brushing... their eyes locked—

"You've got a rebel on your hands."

Deacon's voice shook her from her reverie in time to spy her nephew kicking his mount into a lope in order to overtake the girl ahead of him, breaking not one but two of her instructions.

"Benjy!" she shouted, silently cursing herself for losing focus. "Trotting only."

"But I want to race," the boy complained.

"Maybe at the end of class, if you behave."

He pouted but did as he was told and pulled back on the reins, his small body bouncing up and down in the saddle as the horse's gait slowed. Luckily, Skittles was just about the laziest horse at the arena and more than happy to forfeit the race.

Ah, Benjamin. He was his mother's child and liked nothing better than to test everyone's patience. Liberty couldn't say whether or not he resembled his father. Cassidy had taken a page from their mother's book and refused to reveal the man's identity. Liberty supposed her sister had her reasons, but without knowing them, she only felt sorry for the man who wasn't getting an opportunity to be a part of his son's life.

What about Mercer? Did she feel sorry for him, too? He hadn't gotten to be a part of his grandson's life either. Or Cassidy's. Or hers.

Liberty bit down on her lower lip again. It was all so darn confusing.

The lesson continued for another ten minutes. When it was over, she headed to the gate and opened it so her students could exit the arena—single file except for Benjamin, who couldn't resist cutting up one last time. As if connected by a string, the parents moved in a group to greet their children and oversee unsaddling the horses. When they were done, they'd walk with their children around the grounds, giving the horses a brief cooldown.

Some of the horses belonged to the Becketts and were used by students at various skill levels. A few were privately owned and either boarded at the arena or were transported in for lessons by trailer. Liberty herself owned three horses, including one very young, very green mare she hoped to eventually use for equine endurance competitions.

She hadn't been bitten as strongly by the rodeo bug as the rest of her family. Though she'd competed in barrel racing up through high school, her passions were team penning and trail riding. At every opportunity, at any time of year, she rode into the nearby hills and mountains, seeking the most obscure, roughest terrain she could find.

"Come on, Benjy," she called, her patience all but used up.

It was her job to make sure her nephew took care of his horse, just like the rest of the students. Afterward, Tatum had volunteered to keep an eye on Benjamin until the family meeting was over. Her children were close in age to him and the four frequently played together.

Liberty was sure Cassidy's intentions were to keep her son out of Mercer's sights. To that end, Liberty would make certain they walked Skittles behind the barn. "This way, Benjy."

The boy was far more interested in entertaining his fellow students and refused to listen to his taskmaster aunt.

Deacon appeared from nowhere and fell into step beside Liberty. "Mind if I tag along?"

Please, tell her it wasn't so. "What do you want, Deacon?"

"If you must know, Mercer asked that I make sure you're at the meeting."

"He thinks I'll miss it?"

"He knows you're...miffed at him."

"Miffed?"

"His words."

"Well, he's wrong." Liberty walked faster. "I'm not miffed. I'm furious. And hurt. With good reason, I might add."

Deacon easily kept pace. "Don't judge your father too harshly, Liberty. His intentions are good."

"Of course you'd say that, you're his attorney."

"Give him time. There's a lot to sort out."

"That's putting it mildly."

They caught up with Benjamin at last. Skittles plodded along behind him, the reins dragging on the ground.

"Benjy, pick up the reins. What if Skittles runs off?"

"She won't go nowhere."

He was right, but that wasn't the point.

"It's a bad habit to get into. Horses are animals and unpredictable." Liberty stood, her right foot tapping, and waited for her nephew to do as he was told. "Benjamin."

Finally, he bent over and snatched the reins. As he did, his hat fell off. "Shoot!"

At least he hadn't cussed. Benjamin was growing up around cowboys, and his language tended to be a bit riper than his mother liked.

Dropping the reins he'd picked up seconds earlier, he scrambled for the hat and again muttered, "Shoot."

Deacon stepped forward, retrieved the reins and handed them to Benjamin. "That's a fine mount you have there."

The boy's gaze went up…and up. He seemed to notice Deacon for the first time.

"Her name's Skittles." Benjamin accepted the reins from Deacon's considerably larger outstretched hand.

Liberty's heart beat erratically. This wasn't going as planned. She'd wanted to keep her nephew out of sight and under wraps. Cassidy wouldn't want him drawn into the situation with Mercer until everything was resolved. *If* it was resolved.

"I know," Deacon said. "I remember her."

"You do?" The boy's eyes widened. "How?"

"I worked here a long time ago. Before you were born. Skittles was one of the horses the pickup men regularly used. I even rode her now and again."

"Really? My mom says she's old."

"Older than you, for sure. But she's a good horse. Treat her right, and she'll be your best friend."

Liberty's nerves were about to tear her in two. She had to get Benjamin away before something happened.

"I'll meet you at the house." She took her nephew's hand. "I promise to be at the meeting. You don't have to baby-sit me."

Before Deacon could answer, Liberty's worst fears came true. The office door opened and, as if in slow motion, Mercer stepped outside, accompanied by her mother. His gaze went right to Benjamin, and he started forward. Sunny called after him, but he ignored her, making a beeline for Benjamin.

No, no, no! Liberty instinctively stepped in front of the boy. It was no use.

"Liberty." Mercer was beaming by the time he reached them. "Is this my grandson?"

Benjamin looked up at her, his small brow knit with confusion. "Who's he?"

The next instant, Cassidy rounded the corner of the barn and broke into a run. She wasn't fast enough.

"Mercer, don't," Liberty said, her voice a hoarse whisper.

"This might not be the best time," Deacon added.

Mercer had eyes and ears only for Benjamin. He went down on one knee in front of the boy. As Cassidy skidded to a stop in front of them, he said, "How do you do, young man? I'm your grandfather."

IN THE SPAN OF a single heartbeat, everything went from slow motion to lightning speed. Cassidy swooped up her son and hurried him to the office where, Liberty suspected, he'd be deposited in Tatum's care. Mercer rose, disappointment written all over his face. Sunny called over one of the ranch hands and instructed, "Take care of Skittles for me, please."

At that moment, droplets of rain started to fall.

"Shall we head into the house?" Deacon posed the question more as a statement. When Mercer hesitated, his gaze lingering on the closed office door, Deacon helped him along with a tilt of his head in the direction of the house. "I have an appointment after this."

Mercer's shoulders slumped. "Just wanted to meet my grandson."

"You will. Later. Don't push it." Deacon's voice was mild but firm.

The older man ambled toward the John Deere all-terrain Gator they used to drive between the house and arena. Sunny went, too.

Liberty watched the entire exchange with interest. Mercer's acute disappointment appeared genuine. And

Deacon...this was hardly the shy, keep-to-himself teenager she remembered. He'd taken control of what could have been an explosive situation with tact and authority.

Apparently, he wasn't done. Before Liberty could object, he grasped her by the elbow and briskly steered her across the open area. "Come on."

Since they wouldn't be riding with her parents on the Gator—it held only two people—the only other choice was to walk. She'd assumed Cassidy would be the one making the two hundred yard trek with her. Not Deacon.

"What about my sister?"

He didn't miss a beat. "She'll be along shortly."

No argument there. Cassidy wouldn't forgo this meeting for anything, even a near disastrous run-in between Mercer and her son. Both sisters were eager to know what the future held for them.

Staring at Deacon's fingers resting possessively on her elbow, she said, "I won't run away. I promise."

"I believe you."

"You can let go of me."

"Could."

But, obviously, *wouldn't*. She had to admit the sensation of him touching her bare skin wasn't unpleasant. Far from it, actually. When she was thirteen, she'd dreamed of this very scenario. Only then, they were walking in the moonlight instead of a light sprinkle of rain and not on their way to a meeting guaranteed to be stress filled. Oh, and he wasn't representing her father, either.

Inside the house, the group convened in the living room. The rain picked up, creating a loud ruckus as it pummeled the roof. Thunder boomed.

"Help yourself," Sunny said. She'd arranged for a selection of beverages. Ice water, iced tea and sodas. No afternoon snacks, however. She wasn't feeling that amicable.

"You still have this." Mercer stood in front of an antique pine side table Liberty had seen so often she'd taken it for granted.

"Of course." Her mother settled on the far end of the couch, a glass of iced tea balanced in her hands.

"It was my grandmother's," he told Liberty. "She gave it to us when your mother and I got married. Along with that silver tea set over there." He hitched his chin at the side table in the corner.

Liberty's breath caught. Her mother had always said the pieces were passed down from one family member to the next. But not *Mercer*'s family.

"I—I didn't realize," she stammered, wondering when the surprises were going to end.

An awkward tension descended on the room as everyone jockeyed for seats. Liberty and Mercer both went for the couch and the empty place next to her mother. He won. Liberty refused to sit next to Deacon on the love seat—too reminiscent of the Flat Iron Restaurant.

That left only two spots, the more coveted one across the room. Rather than make a big production, she chose the chair adjacent to Deacon. Surely the meeting wouldn't last more than an hour. She could manage the proximity to him for that long.

The existing tension promptly escalated when Cassidy arrived, sans Benjamin. Face flushed, clothes damp and invisible daggers shooting from her eyes, she took the last vacant seat, then lit into Mercer.

"You are not to speak to my son without my permission and without me being present. Do you understand?"

"My apologies," he said, his expression sincere. "I thought you'd told him."

Liberty attempted to steel her defenses on the chance he was manipulating them. It was harder than it should have been.

"Are we ready to begin?" Deacon removed a stack of

legal-sized papers from his briefcase and distributed a set to everyone in the room. "I'll give you a few minutes to look these over."

Liberty stared at the pages in her hand. The words "Partnership Agreement" were typed in big bold letters, along with a red stamp declaring the document to be a draft.

Deacon started out by summarizing the agreement. In a nutshell, Liberty's mother would continue to run the administrative and financial side of the arena business. Mercer would be in charge of the livestock and bucking contracts.

"What about Walter?" Cassidy asked.

Liberty was also curious. Their current livestock foreman had been with them for nearly thirty years, promoted from assistant foreman after Mercer left.

"He's retiring next spring," Deacon said. "That's been his plan all along."

Being a regular at the arena, Deacon would know. Walter often chatted about him and his wife moving to Wickenburg in order to be closer to their son.

"So, you're getting rid of him early." Cassidy glared at Mercer.

"Not at all." He addressed her for the first time since she'd lit into him about her son. "Walter can stay on until he's ready. I'm counting on him to show me the ropes."

"But you're demoting him."

"His title and pay will remain the same," Deacon responded. "But he'll report to Mercer rather than your mother."

"What's *his* title?" There was no doubt to whom Cassidy referred.

"What it's always been. Co-owner."

That didn't go over well. Cassidy stiffened, and Sunny's lips thinned. Liberty caught herself balling her hands into tight fists.

"Your duties and those of Liberty will remain the same,"

Deacon continued. "You'll report to both your parents for their respective areas of operation. The rest of the staff will, as well. There's a detailed listing of job duties in section three, article five."

The rustle of papers filled the room as everyone flipped pages. After a moment of silence, the room erupted as question after question was fired at Deacon. He responded with clear, precise explanations. Occasionally, Mercer interjected. Most of their answers weren't well received. Cassidy and Sunny constantly talked over each other.

Liberty alone was quiet, overwhelmed by the loud voices and the document's wordy legalese. When had it stopped raining?

At the mention of her name, her head shot up. "I beg your pardon."

"Tomorrow morning." Her mother laid the agreement aside. "After your lessons."

"What about tomorrow morning?"

"Showing Deacon around. I can't make it. The hay delivery is scheduled for nine. After that, Mercer and I will be meeting with Dr. Houser."

The Becketts' veterinarian. He regularly visited to check on all new livestock, administer vaccinations, deworm the horses and calves, treat injuries and a dozen other reasons. Mercer, as the head of livestock, would want to oversee both the hay delivery and Dr. Houser's visit.

Was her mother possibly okay with all of this?

"Deacon's been coming here for months," Liberty protested. "He doesn't need to be *shown around*."

"A tour of the operations," he said.

Clearly, she'd missed a vital part of the discussion.

"Before I can finalize the partnership agreement," he explained, "I need to have a thorough understanding of how each individual aspect of the arena operations functions and what kind of revenue it generates." He consulted his tablet. "Rodeos. Livestock leasing. Horse boarding. Classes. Teaching clinics. Team penning and bucking competitions. I'll also require access to the office and all the files. Your mother said you'd be available."

"Me," she answered flatly.

His brows rose. "Is there a problem?"

"Problem?" This could not be happening to her. "Let's see. Where do I begin?"

Chapter Four

"Awful late for a ride, isn't it?"

Ignoring Mercer, Liberty slipped the cinch strap through the buckle, pulled tight and fed the prongs into the holes. The mare shifted her weight, adjusting to the saddle and cinch.

"Though I suppose it does stay light till past eight these days," he said, his tone casual as his gaze searched the horizon. "But it might rain again. Those dogs of yours are going to get wet."

Three of the ranch dogs had followed Liberty and were lying against the barn wall in a small patch of shade, their tongues lolling and their sides heaving as they panted.

"Won't be the first time."

She didn't care if the skies opened and released a torrent. She was not staying here a minute longer. Besides, she always carried a slicker in her saddlebag, along with matches, a flashlight, tarp and twine.

"What do you want, Mercer?"

He stepped closer, well into her personal space. Liberty tried not to react. Her fingers moved quickly, checking snaps and ties and stirrup lengths.

"To apologize." Removing his cowboy hat, he swept a hank of gray hair from his forehead.

"For what?" There were so many infractions to choose from.

He placed a hand on the mare's nose, murmuring reassurances when she snorted. "She's a dandy. Yours?"

"Mine."

Liberty had tethered her mare to a hitching rail outside the tack room. From her vantage point, she could see the entire arena.

The place was alive with activity. The fierce but short rainstorm had cooled the temperature enough that people were arriving in droves. Cowboys practicing their calf-roping or steer-wrestling skills, pleasure riders exercising their horses and barrel racers attempting to improve on their times.

"You have a good eye." Mercer studied the mare from nose to tail. "Is she well broke?"

"Broke enough."

He chuckled.

"If you're through, then—"

"Give me a minute, okay? You're not the easiest person in the world to have a conversation with."

A sob rose inside her. She swallowed before it escaped. "Maybe because the first time we met you told me you were threatening my mother with a lawsuit."

"Deacon has already read me the riot act over that."

He did? Liberty just assumed Mercer had spoken on his attorney's advice. "Well deserved."

"That man likes you."

"Which, unless I'm wrong, has nothing to do with your apology."

"No, but as his client, I don't want—"

It was Liberty's turn to cut him off. "You have nothing to worry about." And he didn't.

Grabbing a hoof pick off the railing, she bent and lifted the mare's front foot, bracing it above her knee. The mare's muscles tensed, then she tossed her head in an angry jerk. Though improving daily, she still didn't like having her hooves cleaned.

"You're a lot like your mother." Mercer replaced his hat on his head. "And like me, too. I'm thinking you inherited the best from both of us."

"I'm not anything like you."

"You know good horseflesh when you see it." He patted the mare's rump. "And, from what I'm told, you have a natural way with anything on four legs."

As if to prove his point, one of the dogs stood, bowed in a deep stretch, then came over to sit beside her and gaze up with adoring eyes. Liberty barely refrained from groaning with exasperation.

"Always had a fondness for dogs myself." Mercer slapped his thigh. All three dogs responded by mobbing him for attention.

Traitors, Liberty thought grumpily, and moved to the mare's back hooves.

"I should have been more tactful when I told you about your mother and I and the arena."

Liberty stopped to glare at him. "That's what you're apologizing for? A lack of tactfulness."

"I'm not sorry I came back."

"What about using me to get at Mom?"

"I prefer to think of it as killing two birds with one stone."

"Oh, my, God." She emphasized each word. "You are the most self-centered, self-serving individual I've ever met."

"I love your mother."

"You what!" The hoof pick fell from Liberty's grasp. She retrieved it with limp, clumsy fingers.

"Should I say, I've never stopped loving her. It's why I came back."

"Really. Then why haven't you returned before now?"

"We've known each other since we were kids. I grew up half a mile down the road from her."

"Wait, wait, wait." Liberty nipped his trip down memory lane in the bud. "How exactly is threatening Mom with a lawsuit, then muscling your way into our lives, a display of your enduring love?"

"Like I said, your mother is one stubborn lady."

Liberty couldn't argue that. Her mother's supply of forgiveness was nonexistent where Mercer's drinking was concerned.

"It was easy enough to keep tabs on her. We have a lot of mutual friends in the business. I knew she hadn't remarried, or even dated much. Made me think she might still love me, too." He released a long, drawn-out breath. "The timing was never right."

Funny, now that Liberty thought about it, her mother had cited the same excuse about timing when Liberty demanded to know why she'd been lied to.

How convenient. Seems she'd been a victim of bad timing her entire life.

"You saw a chance to come back when I contacted you."

He nodded. "That I did."

"You don't really want to get to know me." It surprised her how much the realization hurt. "You only want to reconcile with Mom."

"Liberty, honey, that couldn't be further from the truth."

"You just said it." Tears pricked her eyes. Damn. She did not want to break down in front of him.

"I do want to reconcile with Sunny. And since she would barely speak to me, I had no choice but to muscle my way in." He took a step toward her and raised his arm. When she retreated, he let his hand drop. "Make no mistake, nothing is more important to me than finding out I have another daughter and getting to know her."

She wanted to believe him. The little girl inside her was

ready to rush into his arms like she had in the restaurant. She held back. The grown woman in her was still angry, and justifiably so.

"Maybe we could talk." He appealed to her with a charmingly boyish grin that must have won her mother over in many an argument. "When you're not heading off on a ride."

Was he trying to wangle an invitation to join her? Not happening! Not today, anyway. But she would like to talk to him, she realized. Later, when she felt less vulnerable.

"I'll think about it." She removed the bridle from where it hung by the saddle horn and slipped it onto the mare's broad head.

"I'll be here. Whenever you're ready."

With that, Mercer strode down the barn aisle and disappeared through the office door. She watched him, then continued staring at empty space for several seconds.

"This is stupid." Untying the mare with a tug on the lead rope, she settled the reins and swung up into the saddle.

She rode by the office at a slow jog. Deacon's truck was gone from the parking area. Apparently, he really had had an appointment after the family meeting.

That man likes you.

Mercer's comment played over and over in her head like one of those songs you couldn't shake. She ignored it—or tried to. If Deacon did like her, why take on Mercer as a client?

Maybe because she hadn't done more than flirt with him. That wasn't enough of a romantic overture for him to turn down a potentially lucrative business arrangement. As he'd said, he had a brand-new office to pay for and clients weren't beating down his door.

She aimed the mare toward the pastures behind the barn and the gate leading to the vast expanse of federal land bordering the Becketts' property. Beyond that, the mountain trails beckoned with their incredible view of Roosevelt Lake. She wouldn't go far, not with dusk falling in a couple of hours.

Just long enough to dispel the confusion currently clouding her thinking.

Without dismounting, she guided the mare parallel to the gate, leaned down and, with one hand, unhooked the latch. On the other side, she repeated the process and closed the gate, pleased at the mare's performance. Months of training were paying off.

The latch had hardly slipped into place when her phone buzzed, alerting her to a text message. She removed the phone from her shirt pocket and read the display. The message was from Deacon.

Didn't have a chance to confirm before you left. See you tomorrow morning at 11:00.

She hated that a ripple of anticipation swept through her before she came to her senses and deleted the message without responding.

"LIBERTY ISN'T HERE YET." There was no mistaking the irritation in Tatum Mayweather's voice.

Deacon infused a dose of honey in his. "I'm early."

"Almost an hour."

He lowered his briefcase onto the seat of the closest visitor chair. The leather was hand tooled, the briefcase custom-made. A pair of locking steer horns branded onto the front was his own design. "Thought I'd get a head start on reviewing the arena records."

Tatum reached for the desk phone. "I'll page Sunny."

"No need. I don't want to interrupt her and Mercer." He flashed his most sincere smile. "There's no problem, is there? Sunny did authorize you to give me access to the files."

"Yes…"

"Good," he said, as if all was settled. "I'd like to start with the personnel records. Are they here?" He indicated the lateral file cabinet he'd leaned against the other day.

"No. Those are stored in Sunny's office." With painstaking hesitancy, Tatum opened the center drawer of her desk and dug out a small silver key attached to an oversize ring.

Deacon held out his hand. "I'll try not to disturb you."

She hesitated, not yet ready to surrender the key. "I should call Sunny."

"Go ahead. I'll wait." He sat in the second visitor chair and stretched his legs out, attempting to appear calm, cool and collected.

He'd deviated from the agreed-upon arrangement, and Tatum knew it. Sunny was supposed to be present during any examination of the records. If not her, then Liberty. He'd planned to arrive early, while Sunny and Mercer were busy with Dr. Houser and Liberty was running errands. He'd wanted time alone with the personnel records and had taken the chance he could buffalo his way past the Becketts' dedicated office manager.

Tatum punched a number into the phone. "Hi, Sunny. Sorry to bother you." She quickly explained the situation. "Okay. Yeah, sure." She fired a stern glance at Deacon. "I don't think so." After another brief exchange and pause, she hung up. "Sunny says it's all right."

Tension flowed from Deacon in waves. He was going to pull this off. "Thank you."

Rather than give him the key, Tatum accompanied him into Sunny's office and opened the file cabinet herself. "Everything you need is in the top drawer. You can sit at Sunny's desk."

Deacon quickly perused the row of manila files with

their color-coded labels. There were no more than twelve or fifteen. "How far back do these go?"

"Current employees only, if that's what you're asking."

"What about former employees? Where are those files?"

"Archived," Tatum answered tightly.

"If it's not too much trouble…"

"They're stored in the attic above the garage." Her tone implied retrieving the files would be a *great deal* of trouble.

Deacon had anticipated just such a roadblock and tried another approach. "What about electronic copies of the records?"

"On a backup hard drive. I'd have to restore the information year by year."

He began to suspect the office manager was intentionally waylaying him. Her next remark, however, had him reconsidering.

"I do have copies of the annual W-2 wage statements for the last ten years."

"That'll help. Thank you."

Walter was the only current employee who'd been around at the time of Ernie Tuckerman's accident. More than once, Deacon had discreetly prodded the livestock foreman for information. The rodeo world was small but apparently not that small. Walter hadn't kept in touch with any of the arena's former employees or customers who'd moved from Reckless, other than when they returned for a rodeo or the annual Wild West Days. The few vague leads he'd supplied failed to pan out.

No doubt some of the people Deacon sought still lived in town. The arena records would enable him to narrow his search. He didn't have to look far for Ernie Tuckerman. Deacon had spotted him frequently going into the market or standing on a corner. Talk was Deacon's former rival lived hand to mouth in a single-wide trailer on the edge of town and didn't get out much. His pronounced limp ripped the heart clean out of Deacon, as did his thin, haggard appearance.

Seeing the other man's suffering only strengthened Deacon's resolve to find the person responsible for the accident. As much for Ernie as himself. They'd both been wronged and had been paying the price for too long.

"Wait here." With a toss of her long black hair, Tatum went to the storage closet and unearthed a bulging box from its farthest recesses. She dropped the box on Sunny's desk and said, "Anything else?"

"Not at the moment." He stopped her when she reached the door. "I saw you have a new picture of your kids on your desk."

"I took them to the zoo last month." She smiled tentatively.

"Nice shot."

Encouraged, Deacon sat in Sunny's chair. Powering up his tablet, he started on the oldest W-2 wage statements first. Halfway through the box, he'd managed to plug several names and addresses into his tablet. Seemed Sunny was good at gathering updated addresses when a W-2 was returned as undeliverable.

"What are you doing?"

Liberty. From the sound of it, she stood in the doorway. Deacon could feel her stare boring straight through him.

"My job." He forced himself not to deviate from his task.

She moved into the office, prompting him to at last glance up. She wore a severe scowl—which was a real shame. She was far too pretty not to be smiling all the time.

"You're not supposed to be here without my mother or me."

"True. But Sunny gave her permission. You can ask your office manager."

"I will." Liberty came closer. "When she's off the phone."

Interesting. She'd come charging in here without first checking with Tatum. He took enjoyment in being the cause of Liberty's hair-trigger reaction. Any emotion, even a negative one, showed she wasn't immune to him.

"I was early," he said.

"Figures."

"Thought I'd spend the time getting a jump on the arena records."

She angled her head sideways to read the file lying open in front of him. "By looking at old W-2s?"

"How much you pay your employees is relevant to the operations."

"From five years ago?"

"I'm tracking wage history."

"Hmm." Her eyes narrowed with suspicion.

Again, Deacon was struck with the conviction that she should be smiling as often as possible.

Closing the file, he powered off his tablet before she could read what he'd entered. "If you're ready now, we can tour the grounds. I'll finish this later."

"When my mother's done with the vet," she reiterated, "and available to oversee you."

"Sure." Deacon wasn't worried.

He had enough names and addresses to start his search. And he'd find ways to dig into more arena records, even with Sunny or Liberty watching his every move.

Hopefully it would be Liberty. She could watch his every move anytime she wanted. And he'd watch hers in return. Kind of like he was doing now.

Chapter Five

Deacon and Liberty passed through the front office on their way to the barn. Tatum was off the phone, but Liberty didn't stop and confirm that Deacon had indeed obtained Sunny's permission to nose through the files. He awarded himself a mental check mark in the plus column.

"Where shall we start?" Liberty asked.

He glanced down the main aisle. "Since we're here, how about with horse boarding?"

"Sure." She shrugged her consent.

Shifting his briefcase to the other hand, he followed her.

Liberty paused, her eyes fastened on the briefcase. "Very nice."

"A gift from my mother when I graduated law school."

"She has good taste."

"In some things."

Not in men. But Liberty was already aware of that, along with most of the town. His parents' reputations, as much as the accident, could account for Deacon's slow-to-take-off legal practice.

"Looks expensive. You might want to leave it in the office."

"I'll drop it off in my truck later." There were several important and confidential documents inside the briefcase. Deacon would rather be safe than sorry.

They stopped in front of Deacon's two horses. Liberty absently combed her fingers through the gelding's fetlock. "You already know how much we charge for the indoor box stalls, seeing as you pay for two of them."

"How many of the fifty stalls are rented out?"

"Thirty-five at last count."

Deacon didn't take notes. This kind of information was available in the records. Mostly, he was trying to get a general feel for the arena's business operations. Hard numbers could come later.

Strolling the row of indoor stalls, they discussed feeding schedules, quantity of feed, prices, availability and storage. As they neared the sheds, the strong aroma of fresh-cut hay triggered an onslaught of memories. How many bales had Deacon stacked during his youth? Too many to count. If he concentrated, he could feel the baling wire cutting into his palms and the thick welts rising in spite of the leather gloves he'd worn.

Sunny had worked him hard, yet those two years had been the happiest time of his youth. The *only* happy time in his life until his twenties when he entered college.

"We purchase hay in the summer," Liberty said, not noticing his momentary lapse. "It should last the entire year, barring any problems like mold or damage from pests."

"Isn't July when prices are at their lowest?"

"It's also right after the Rough Riders rodeo."

Made sense, he thought. The rodeo was one of the Easy Money's best attended events and produced the surplus of cash needed to purchase such a large quantity of hay.

At Deacon's request, they headed toward the outdoor stalls and pastures. The horses there paid little attention to the two of them. Standing quietly with heads hung low, they swished their tails at the flies. The mares and foals in the pasture sniffed the ground in search of tidbits. A lazy pair stood head to toe in the marginally cooler shade of an awning.

"How's your mom's doing?" Liberty asked.

Despite the earlier mention of his mother, the question hit Deacon like a sucker punch to the gut. "Same as always."

"Do you see her often?"

He squinted in an easterly direction. "Globe isn't that far away." His parents had moved to Reckless's closest and considerably larger neighboring town a year after Deacon ran away. He sometimes wondered if they weren't afraid of him returning to Reckless and had moved because of it.

"That's not what I'm asking," Liberty said.

"Only if I absolutely have to."

Like when his mother called him, hinting for money or a favor. He usually granted the favor. Money, that was different. He'd buy her groceries or put gas in her car or pay her utility bill before he'd hand over cash. Carol McCrea would simply waste it. Lottery tickets, pedicures, magazine subscriptions, you name it. Vital necessities were last on her priority list.

"And I don't talk to my dad at all, if you were going to ask that next."

"Sorry," Liberty said. "I was just being polite."

Deacon regretted his terseness. "No, I'm sorry. I shouldn't take my screwed-up parents out on you."

"When it comes to screwed-up parents, mine set the bar."

He slowed his steps. "We're quite the pair, I suppose."

"At least you knew your dad, and he was around every day."

"I'd have been better off without him."

"Don't say that. Growing up without a dad is hard."

He felt sorry for her. But growing up without a father couldn't have been worse than having Henry McCrea for one. He hadn't beaten or abused his wife and children or mistreated them in the slightest. He would have had to acknowledge their existence for that.

Deacon's father was only interested in which of the town ladies, or those in nearby Globe, he could sweet-talk into bed. They were the ones he spent his money on, the ones on whom he lavished his attention. Most tired of him when he wouldn't divorce his wife. Frankly, Deacon wasn't sure why his father hadn't walked out on his family. He surely didn't love them.

As a result, Deacon's mother had vented her frustration and unhappiness by constantly berating and belittling Deacon and his sister. Misery needs company, and his mother guaranteed she had plenty of it. Had either of Deacon's parents cared a lick about anyone other than themselves, his acute reading disability might have been diagnosed and treated years earlier, and he wouldn't have earned the nickname Einstein.

He also might not have been blamed for an accident he didn't cause and fired from a job he loved.

He'd left Reckless soon after the accident, though at seventeen he was considered a runaway. Just like his sister two summers before him. Only she'd traveled much farther, to California, and would likely never return. Or so she told him during their infrequent conversations.

A loud ruckus had Deacon and Liberty turning to investigate. One of the hands was driving a tractor toward the arena and pulling a grader blade behind him. Kenny—a freckled-face high school junior—waved. He might have been Deacon at that age, only Deacon wouldn't have done anything as overtly friendly as wave. He'd have nodded stoically, the most he could muster.

Except when he saw Liberty. Then, he'd have blushed beet-red beneath his tan. It wouldn't have mattered that she was just a kid. She'd been smitten with him, he could tell, and her crush had embarrassed him to his core.

No more. If he drove by her today, he'd stop the tractor and ask her to hop on.

They meandered to the far pasture that held the bucking stock. Almost immediately, the horses plodded over. Bucking stock could be quite tame outside the arena, depending on their personalities. Inside the arena was another story. They were trained to do a job, and if the owners were lucky, they did it well, earning back their keep along with a tidy profit.

"We have twenty-seven altogether," Liberty said, anticipating Deacon's next question. "Two are currently residing in the infirmary."

"What happened?"

Liberty leaned her forearms on the pasture railing. She instantly became the object of much sniffing and nudging. "Biggie Size has a laceration on his knee, and Calamity Jane's on a diet."

"A diet?" Deacon chuckled.

"She's hog fat." Liberty didn't laugh in return. "It's interfering with her ability to buck."

"That is serious."

"She's been one of our top earners. Until she became such a glutton."

"Tell me about the bucking stock side of the operation," Deacon said.

"You know. You were a wrangler."

"Things have changed since then."

"Obviously, we supply the horses, calves and steer for our own rodeos. No bulls. Those, we lease. Usually from the Lost Dutchman Rodeo Company out of Apache Junction."

There was pride in her voice and with good reason. Under Sunny's direction, the Easy Money had earned a stellar reputation. They were also the only bucking stock operation Deacon knew of to be run exclusively by women.

No more. Mercer's return changed that. Would it affect their business? Being woman-run had given the Becketts a certain advantage with some rodeo organizations and associations and a disadvantage with others.

"Calamity Jane being your one exception," Deacon said. At Liberty's puzzled expression, he added, "She's too fat to be the best."

His teasing remark earned him a hint of a smile. Good. She wasn't made of stone after all.

Loud bawling greeted their arrival at the calf pens. Typical. The sight of a human almost always triggered that reaction in bovine. Regardless of the time of day, the calves associated people with being fed. The appearance of Deacon and Liberty started a chain reaction in the herd.

Before long, the calves were bunched together at the fence. In the next pen over, the steer weren't any better and made a similar feed-me-feed-me fuss.

"You never told me goodbye when you left," Liberty said.

He hadn't seen that remark coming and needed a moment to recover before replying.

"It was a quick decision. I didn't say goodbye to a lot of people."

Including his parents. Deacon had thrown a few belongings into a backpack and hit the road, catching a ride to Phoenix with Lenny Faust, owner of the local Ship-With-Ease store.

"I never believed for one second you left that gate unlatched."

He met Liberty's gaze. "You're the only one."

"Everyone assumed you were guilty when you took off like that."

"They assumed I was guilty the moment Ernie Tuckerman accused me from his hospital bed." Resentment rang in Deacon's voice. "Your mother among them."

"It was a rough time for her."

"Her? Your mother's accusations made sure I'd never work in Reckless again."

"She didn't accuse you."

"She fired me, which sent a pretty strong message. She refused to talk to me after the accident or give me a chance to defend myself."

Liberty had the decency to look ashamed. "The accident could have put us out of business."

"Yeah, who cares about one dumb seventeen-year-old kid?"

"It wasn't like that, Deacon." She touched his hand and let her fingers linger.

He didn't want to be angry anymore. Not with her lightly caressing his knuckles. Easier said than done. Deacon had spent a lot of years cultivating his anger. It would take more than a small show of sympathy from Liberty to vanquish it.

Her touch grew stronger. Bolder. The pressure increasing. Then again, maybe his imagination was running away with him. It was possible. Something about Liberty made him feel emotions he'd thought long dead. See possibilities rather than limitations.

"If you had said goodbye, I would have…"

"What, Liberty?" He leaned closer. Only an inch or two. Enough to drown in the vivid blue of her eyes.

"I don't know. Gone to my mother. Pleaded on your behalf."

"You didn't?" Not that he'd expected that from anyone. After her claim that she'd believed in his innocence, however, he'd hoped she might have supported him.

"What was the point? You left."

He withdrew his hand. "Let me get this straight. You didn't defend me to your family because I didn't say goodbye."

"I was a kid."

They both were. And in Deacon's case, he'd been forced to grow up fast.

"I did not leave that gate open," he repeated, "and I'm going to prove it."

"How?"

Before he could go into detail, a large, shiny new pickup truck pulled up to the calf pens and braked to a stop. Deacon recognized the driver—Tom Pratt, professional cowboy and instructor for tonight's roping clinic. The door flew open, and the man stepped out. He was here ahead of time to meet with Sunny and set up before the clinic started.

"Howdy," he called, and ambled toward them.

"We're not done talking about this, Deacon," Liberty whispered before meeting her visitor halfway.

He didn't think they were, either.

MORE THAN THREE DOZEN people had signed up for the roping clinic. A long night loomed ahead for all the Becketts. They'd be lucky to finish by ten, which meant Liberty wouldn't get to bed until eleven, only to have her alarm go off at the crack of dawn.

She was helping Cassidy collect last-minute registrations and process paperwork. The task wasn't consuming enough to take her mind off Deacon and their earlier conversation.

He wanted to clear his name. She sympathized with him, supported him, but what did that say about the two of them? Was there even a her and him to consider?

"Next," Cassidy called through the window. "Hey there, Cal." She beamed at the young cowboy.

It was nice to see her sister smile for a change. She'd been a grouch for days now. Unfortunately, Cassidy's improved mood didn't affect Liberty's sour one.

They were in the registration booth beneath the announcer's stand, which was just large enough to hold four warm bodies, a desk, chair and overhead cupboards stocked with supplies. There was also a safe tucked behind the desk, though money didn't remain there for long. It was quickly transferred to a second safe inside the house.

The Becketts didn't like thinking poorly of their customers or employees, but, sadly, thefts occurred on rare occasion, and they couldn't be too careful.

During their annual rodeos, two horse auctions and various roping, bucking and team penning competitions, the computer was on and the laser printer constantly spewing pages. Not today and not for a simple clinic. There were no scores to tabulate, no bids to record and no times to track.

There wasn't much paperwork to process, either. Before long, Liberty and her sister would be done. Then, the two of them would be on standby during the clinic, helping out in whatever capacity they were needed. Bringing fresh calves from the pens. Fetching equipment. Refilling the cooler with ice and water. Taking pictures, which would then be posted on their website to advertise the next clinic.

When it was over and the arena regraded in preparation for tomorrow's activities, she'd be free to dwell on Deacon without any of those pesky interruptions.

Finally, the last participant left the registration booth with a "thank you, ma'am" and dashed off to saddle his horse before the clinic started.

Like a lot of the participants tonight, he was from the area and had high hopes of making rodeo his career. The remainder were roping enthusiasts who took their hobby seriously. Of those, a third were women, some of them as good as any man.

Tom Pratt's voice blared from the arena loudspeakers, announcing the start of the clinic. He wore a wireless microphone headset that enabled him to instruct hands-free from either the ground or on horseback.

With the sound of Tom's voice droning in the background, Liberty and Cassidy balanced the registration forms with the cash, checks and credit card receipts they'd collected. Fortunately, everything balanced to the penny on their first try.

Cassidy put the last of the money and receipts in a zippered bank bag. "Want me to run this to the house?"

"Doesn't matter." Liberty closed and locked the cash drawer.

"Okay, I'll go. You can help with the calves."

Liberty had forgotten that Walter was "showing Mercer the ropes" tonight. "I'd rather not, if that's okay."

"You're not the only one who wants to avoid *him.*"

"Please."

"Fine." Cassidy thrust the bank bag at her. "I'll help dear ol' Dad." The endearment wasn't issued with affection.

Liberty pressed her fingers to her forehead and rubbed the ache lodged there. "Sorry. Something's eating at me. Didn't mean to take it out on you."

"News flash, little sis. We all have something eating at us."

Liberty sighed miserably.

"Want to talk about it?"

"Eventually. I'd like to stew for a while first."

Angry as she was at Mercer, she was like any child and wanted her parents together. If she was honest with herself, that was one of the reasons she'd invited him back. Her mother didn't gaze longingly at the picture of them hidden in a drawer because she hated him.

"I saw you and Deacon this afternoon." Cassidy's expression softened. "It looked intense."

"A little."

"Am I right in assuming you two aren't going out anytime soon?"

"We were never going out to begin with."

"Then why are you always panting after him?"

"I do not pant!"

"Last month I saw you cover a hundred yards in ten seconds flat just to make sure he picked you for his team penning partner."

Liberty gasped. "You're making that up."

"Right." Cassidy had the nerve to laugh.

"Argh!" Because she didn't want to engage in yet another childish bickering match with her sister, Liberty refrained from commenting—a feat that required cementing her teeth together

Had she really galloped her horse across the arena? Probably. Definitely. And no more!

"He sure has changed," Cassidy observed. "Who'd have figured him for an attorney?"

"Why not an attorney? He's smart." Liberty's defense of Deacon came out in a rush.

"I didn't say he wasn't." Cassidy locked the booth door behind them.

"You implied it."

"Look, he had trouble with school. Failed most of his classes. Did you ever think he'd wind up with a law degree hanging on his wall? I sure didn't."

"I thought he'd be a champion bull rider."

"There was that," Cassidy said, her tone losing some of its bite.

Liberty's opinion was once shared by many. Deacon had shown considerable promise as a young man. Bull riding. Bronc busting. Steer wrestling. He'd been an all-around cowboy and headed for a state junior rodeo title, along with Ernie Tuckerman. All that changed in the wake of the accident.

"I always wondered what happened to him after he ran away." Cassidy dug the keys to the Gator out of her jeans pocket and tossed them to Liberty. They'd parked the vehicle on the other side of the booth. "Did he ever tell you?"

"Uh-uh." Liberty climbed into the Gator's driver's side.

She'd hinted at the subject a few times, but Deacon remained steadfastly silent. How he had gone from a high school dropout runaway to an attorney must be an incredible story. She was more than curious. She was fascinated.

"Drop me off at the arena on your way to the house," Cassidy instructed, and settled herself in the passenger seat.

Liberty tucked the bank bag in a cubby beneath the dash. "He likes you."

She sat up slowly. Mercer had said almost the exact same thing to her. "He likes a lot of people."

"Not as much as he likes you."

Her sister could be truly tiring at times. "Doesn't make any difference." Glancing backward, she threw the Gator into Reverse and pressed her foot to the gas pedal. "He's Mercer's attorney."

"You should ask him out."

"What! Me? No."

"Think about it." Cassidy held on to the grab bar as they bumped over a pothole. "You could pump him for information on Mercer."

"He won't tell me anything."

"You don't know till you try."

"I know," Liberty countered. "Deacon won't betray his client's trust. He's…honorable."

"He's also a man and susceptible to a woman's charms."

"Forget it." Liberty pulled up alongside the livestock pens. "I already know everything about Mercer's intentions I need to."

"Like what?"

"He still loves Mom."

Cassidy's double take was almost comical. "No way!"

Now that Liberty had let the cat out of the bag, she went with it. "He told me so himself. That's why he came back. To reconcile with her."

"Good Lord." Cassidy slumped against the back of the seat. "What are we going to do?"

Liberty didn't believe the next words out of her mouth. "I think we should help them along."

"Help them?"

"Mom loves him, too."

"She most certainly does not," Cassidy insisted.

"It's been twenty-four years since Mercer left and she's gone on how many dates? Four or five by my count."

"Big deal. I don't date, either."

"Why not?"

Liberty had often contemplated her sister's single status. Benjy's father, whoever he was, must have broken Cassidy's heart. Liberty was the only Beckett woman who went out with any regularity, though seldom seriously. Most of her relationships ended after four to six months. Usually when she finally accepted the guy wasn't *the one*.

Her mother called Liberty a dreamer and accused her of having too high expectations. Liberty couldn't help herself. She wanted to be swept off her feet and fall madly in love.

"Don't try and sidetrack me," Cassidy said. "We're talking about Mom and Mercer. Besides, you hate him."

"I don't. I'm angry at him and his...methods. But in his defense, Mom lied to him, too. He could have felt justified."

"Mom had her reasons."

"I want us to be a family again. At the least, I want to get to know my father."

"He's an alcoholic."

"A former alcoholic. He only started drinking after our grandfather died."

"That's not an excuse."

"No? Our parents are both alive. We don't know how we'd change if one of them suddenly suffered a fatal heart attack. We might use alcohol as a crutch to cope with our grief."

Cassidy grew quiet. "He was different before the drinking."

"Kind of like he is now?"

"He had no right to speak to Benjy without talking to me first."

"I don't disagree." Liberty lowered her voice. "But he wanted to meet his grandson. Is that a crime?"

"He's pushy."

She could think of a few more colorful adjectives to describe him. Had called Mercer one or two to his face. She could also see his good side. He was charming and witty and a skilled livestock foreman. Liberty had heard many stories about him from the old-timers who hung out at the arena during the rodeos and horse sales. Before the drinking started, he'd been well liked, respected, generous to those he called friends and a devoted husband and father.

"There's a reason our brother chose to live with him," Liberty said firmly.

"He wasn't riding in the truck when Mercer crashed into the well house."

"If Mom and Mercer reconcile, Ryder might come visit us." Liberty had missed growing up with her brother.

"That's the *only* good thing about Mercer returning."

"Mom deserves to be happy. They both deserve a second chance if that's what they want. We should remain open to possibilities."

"Not me."

If that was true, then why hadn't Cassidy gotten out of the Gator?

"You had the chance to grow up with him. For a while. I was denied that."

"He could cost us our business."

"The arena is half his. He won't do anything to sabotage it."

"Because he wants his money."

"Because he wants our mother."

Liberty had grown weary of their constant back and forth and decided to end it. "Think about it, please. I'll see you later."

Again, Cassidy didn't move. "What were you and Deacon talking about earlier?"

Hadn't they also exhausted the topic of her and Deacon? Apparently not. "Horse boarding," Liberty said. "The bucking stock operation."

"And that got heated?"

"It wasn't heated."

"Now who's making up stories?"

"He irritates me sometimes."

"I bet." Cassidy laughed.

"It's not what you think. He isn't interested in me. The conversation was intense because Deacon's an intense guy."

"Would you look at that!"

Cassidy's explosive remark had Liberty popping off the seat and searching for a snake or spider. "What?" she asked, finding nothing.

"Over there." Cassidy jabbed her finger at the south gate.

And there was the source of her sister's distress. Mercer and their mother stood together. *Close* together, their heads bent over something too small for Liberty to see. "So what? They're talking."

"Talking, my ass." Cassidy piled out of the Gator and stormed off.

No doubt about it. Her sister was definitely not open to possibilities.

The drive to the house took only a few minutes, as did placing the bank bag inside the safe. Before long, Liberty was returning to the arena. By then, the roping clinic was well under way. She stopped a moment to watch Tom Pratt demonstrate a new technique.

He stood, twirling a rope high over his head, then tossed

it at a practice dummy. A whizzing sound cut the air as the rope flew. Ten, twenty, thirty feet. It landed squarely on the plastic calf head with a solid thwack.

He pulled the rope taut as if the dummy were a real calf. "The trick is to shift your balance at just the right moment." He leaned to one side and patted his thigh.

"Easy for you," a middle-aged man said from the sidelines.

Tom chuckled good-naturedly and motioned to the man. "Come on. You try."

The man jogged over, and the lesson resumed. Liberty glanced about. Her parents were with Walter at the livestock pens behind the chutes. Cassidy was up in the announcer's booth, probably avoiding Mercer. Liberty decided she'd have a chat with Kenny, the teenager who'd graded the arena while she and Deacon were talking this afternoon.

One conversation led to another, one task became many. Before she quite realized it, three hours had passed and the roping clinic was nearing an end. The spectators in the bleacher were up and on their feet, stretching or repacking their coolers.

Liberty started for the arena gate, intending to open it. She paid no attention to the sound of a nearby vehicle, assuming someone had arrived to pick up a participant.

Wrong.

The sight of Deacon's pickup gave her a start. No, more like a thrill. He hadn't mentioned anything about returning tonight. Especially so late. Yet, here he was.

She waited for him to park and exit his truck. He headed straight for her. The thrill intensified.

"You're late," she said. "The clinic's over."

"You have a few minutes to talk?" He looked so serious. "About what?"

He stopped directly in front of her. She had to lift her chin several inches to meet his gaze. The view along the way wasn't bad. He had a nice chest to go with his broad shoulders. She'd noticed that before—frequently.

"You. Me. Your father," he said.

"Aren't there some sort of attorney-client privileges you're not supposed to violate?"

"Don't worry. It's not that kind of conversation."

"I'm all ears."

"Not here." He took her by the arm and guided her across the open area to the picnic table outside the office.

Liberty swore every pair of eyes in the place tracked their progress. She could only imagine what her mother and sister would say when they heard. Nothing she wasn't already telling herself.

Chapter Six

"If this is about you taking on my father as a client—"

"It isn't." Deacon cut Liberty off before she could finish.

She started to rise. "I think maybe we're done here."

It wasn't his intention to be rude. "I'm sorry. I have a lot on my mind."

"We all do, Deacon."

"You're right." He attempted an appealing smile.

She didn't return it. But neither did she leave.

They were seated at the picnic table, facing out toward the arena, their backs leaning against the tabletop. Liberty had folded her hands neatly in her lap.

Deacon studied her rings. The jade one had caught his attention in the restaurant and earlier today when she'd placed her hand on his arm. He hadn't wanted her to stop there and imagined her fingertips sifting through the hair at his temples right before he pulled her into his arms for a lingering kiss.

"If not Mercer, what do you want to talk about?"

Liberty's question vaporized Deacon's fantasy. Just as well. It could only ever be a fantasy.

"First, I wish I could have told you about working for your father. It wasn't fair to spring the news on you like he did, and I apologize for my part in it."

She mulled that over for a moment. "And the second thing?"

Deacon swallowed and dove in. "I may have been seventeen when I worked for your mother, but I took my job and my responsibility very seriously. She put me in charge of the bulls because she knew how dedicated and conscientious I was."

"Okay."

"I always double-checked the latches and locks on the bulls' pen. Sometimes triple-checked them. I didn't forget the day of the accident. I didn't overlook anything. I didn't get sidetracked. Those gates were closed and locked when I walked away from the pen. More than that, the bulls had eaten and were bedded down for the night. Not riled or agitated."

The Becketts had owned ten bulls at the time. They were housed in an area well separated from the rest of the livestock for obvious reasons. Bulls were dangerous animals. Precautions were taken and strictly enforced. Two gates led to the pen, an exterior one and an interior one with a short corridor connecting them.

While it was possible for someone—Deacon—to forget locking one gate, forgetting both was unlikely. Impossible. He wouldn't have done it. No one in their right mind would have.

"There was no sign of the locks being tampered with," he continued. "And if I didn't do it, and I didn't, then someone deliberately opened the gates after I left."

"Why?" Liberty shook her head. "It makes no sense."

"I've asked myself that same question a thousand times. The only answer I've come up with is that someone wanted me to take the fall."

"Or they had a grudge against Ernie."

Deacon's gaze drifted to the empty bull area on the far side of the arena. Nowadays, it was used only during rodeos to house the leased bulls. "Who knew he'd be standing outside the gate at the exact moment the bulls figured out they could escape?"

"They could have called him over."

"I just can't believe they intended for him to be hurt. That's extreme."

"Why let the bulls out at all?"

"So that I'd be blamed."

At his remark, her demeanor changed. Became less defensive. "My mother shouldn't have assumed it was your fault."

Deacon thought the same, then and now. Sunny's lack of faith in him when he'd been an exemplary employee had wounded him. More than his father's indifference and his mother's selfishness.

"Ernie's accusations were pretty convincing."

"People can be cruel." Liberty moved, and her thigh inadvertently came in contact with Deacon's.

Like before when she'd touched his arm, his train of thought immediately derailed.

Clearing his throat, he said, "Which is why I need to find out who was responsible and expose them. Reckless is a small town. Too many people still believe I'm the one who let the bulls escape. Because of that, they don't trust me, and one thing an attorney needs is the trust of his clients. Without that, I have no hope of building my practice."

"I understand."

Did she? There was so much more he wanted to say. How working with her was another reason he had taken on her father as a client and that he thought about her all the time. Instead, he stuck to the subject at hand. Anything else would only complicate matters.

"What do you remember about the accident?"

"Very little. I was a kid. I didn't get involved with the bucking stock then."

"Your mother always carried a key to the bulls' pen. A second one hung on a rack in the office. That was the key I used. I replaced it when I was done."

"Did you that day?"

"Absolutely. But no one saw me. And it was missing after the accident. Missing and never found. Afterwards, your mother changed the locks."

"The office doors stay open during the workday. Anyone could have walked in and taken the key."

"They would have had to be quick. The bulls escaped not five minutes after I left them."

"Who was here that night?"

"Too many to count," Deacon said. "The Wild West Days Rodeo was the following weekend. A lot of cowboys had signed up for practice. There must have been twenty or thirty that day alone. Plus the wranglers. The bulls were worn-out. It seems strange that one of them would have charged."

"Bulls do get riled at the smallest things."

"Or someone purposely riled them."

"But who?" Liberty repeated. "And why?"

He shrugged. "It could have been a rivalry. I was headed for a state junior rodeo championship. But I wasn't the only one. There were ten or twelve from Reckless alone. Including Ernie."

Cowboys came from as far away as Mesa and Tucson to practice before a rodeo. Pinpointing a single rival, especially one angry or threatened enough to take drastic measures, would be nearly impossible.

"The more I think about it, the more I'm convinced Ernie was the intended target. It just makes sense."

"Except," Liberty countered, "you were a victim of bullying."

"Calling someone names is a lot different than setting out to injure them and possibly others."

"Have you talked to Ernie? Maybe he remembers something."

Deacon chuckled drily.

"Why not?"

"I don't think he'd be willing."

"Don't know if you don't try."

This time his laughter was filled with humor. "You remind me of someone."

"Who?" Her eyes lit up.

Damn, they were blue. And the way she looked at him—if they were a normal couple he'd be making some of those fantasies about her come true.

"A mentor," he said, forcing himself to concentrate. "He helped me out when I really needed it."

"I'd like to hear about him."

"Maybe one day."

More like never. Deacon wasn't about to admit he was the proud owner of a juvenile record or talk about the detention officer who'd changed his life. He was already having enough trouble convincing folks he wasn't responsible for Ernie's misfortune.

"Maybe we could go out for lunch or happy hour."

Had she just suggested a date?

"Seeing as we'll be working together," she clarified.

"Yeah, right." A meeting between business associates. Not a date. Stupid him.

It didn't matter. Deacon would still go. Anywhere or anytime, just for the chance to be in her company.

"I'd better get back to work." She hesitated, almost as if she was waiting for him to insist she stay.

His mind said those exact words. What came out of his mouth was, "What time tomorrow is good for you?"

"Ten-thirty. I'll be done with classes by then."

He didn't suggest that Sunny be the one to babysit him while he reviewed the arena records, and Liberty didn't offer. Deacon tried not to read too much into that and simply counted his lucky stars.

They stood, first her, then him.

He surveyed the nearly empty grounds. "Looks like the roping clinic was a success."

"We're thinking of hosting one every other month. Tom's a popular instructor. We're fortunate to have him."

"I should sign up. I sometimes wish I'd concentrated more on roping and less on steer wrestling."

"But you were good. You'd have won the state championship if you didn't quit."

"I ran away. Not much call for rodeoing on the streets of Phoenix."

"So, that's where you went." She seemed to have forgotten about work.

"For a while." After a few months, he'd wound up in a juvenile detention facility in Mesa. Awful as it was, it had changed his life, setting him on an entirely new course.

"Your parents didn't know where you were," Liberty said. "I asked them."

"They knew. They just didn't want to say." And Deacon didn't blame them. "I haven't wrestled a steer since college."

"I bet you still can." Liberty grinned impishly, and a tiny dimple appeared in the corner of her mouth.

What would it be like to brush his lips across hers? Let them linger on that dimple? Tease her with his tongue until she moaned with need?

Focus, he told himself. "I probably can, but my time would stink."

"Maybe not."

"I'd embarrass myself."

"Come on. Give it a go," she insisted.

"I will. One of these days."

She perked up. "Why not now?"

"It's after ten."

"All the better. No one to see you."

"See me fail."

"You saddle your horse. I'll bring a steer from the pen and operate the chute."

"I'll need a hazer. You can't do both."

"Kenny hasn't left yet."

The teenager who worked part-time and drove the tractor? "How good is he?" Deacon asked, still skeptical.

"Okay in a pinch. I'll ask him." Liberty started off.

"Wait." Deacon took hold of her arm before she got very far. "Why are you even suggesting this?"

"I think you need to prove some things to yourself. And this is one of them."

She had a point. A good one. He was impressed by how well she read him. "All right. But there has to be a prize. It isn't a competition without one."

She eyed him suspiciously. "What do you have in mind?"

"My best time back in the day was three-point-four seconds. I can't come close to that. But I'm pretty sure I can beat twelve seconds."

"And if you do?"

"You agree to help me find out what really happened the day of Ernie's accident and who opened the gates."

She didn't miss a beat. "Ten seconds, and you have a deal."

He laughed then and extended his hand.

She hesitated taking it. "I have my own condition."

This was getting interesting. "Which is…"

"Mercer still loves my mom."

"He told me."

Her brows rose. "He must be serious."

"Evidently."

"I'm thinking my mom also has feelings for him. I'd like to try and help things along."

"Huh. Can I ask why?"

"I want Ryder to come home. And he might if my family's reconciled."

He admired her motives. "I don't know what I can do."

"Get them together. You'll think of something." There was a hint of challenge in her voice, one Deacon responded to.

"All right. We have a deal." Excitement stirred inside him. Too many years had passed since he'd competed.

It was nothing, however, compared to the excitement he felt when he captured Liberty's hand in his and held it tight.

THE MOMENT LIBERTY set foot in the steers' pen, they scattered in every direction. She finally cut one loose and herded it through the gate, down the narrow corridor and toward the chutes. The steer wasn't happy. Neither were his buddies, who resented being disturbed at a time usually reserved for sleeping.

Okay, she admitted it. Steer wrestling with Deacon at nearly ten-thirty at night was one harebrained idea.

It was also great fun and gave her an excuse to help Deacon clear his name. He deserved nothing less for everything he'd been through. What she didn't want was for her mother and sister to think she'd switched sides in this showdown with Mercer.

The steer stopped midway through the corridor and bellowed a loud protest. He was joined by his buddies in the pen. Liberty bit her lip and glanced nervously about. The ruckus would draw the attention of anyone hanging around, and they could do without an audience. Her family in particular.

At the moment, Cassidy and their mother were in the house. Mercer had returned to the Dead Broke Inn, where he was staying until he found a permanent residence or—if his and now Liberty's plan succeeded—moved back into the Becketts' home. All three had been known to return to the arena late at night to check on one thing or another.

"Shoo, shoo." Liberty waved her arms at the steer, relieved when it reluctantly continued on its way.

What did she wish for more? Deacon to win their bet—or her? Deacon winning made more sense. There probably wasn't any way for him to help reconcile her parents, though he did have Mercer's ear and could plant a seed or two.

The steer stopped again outside the chute and stubbornly refused to enter. During a rodeo or practice, he'd have several steer behind him and two or three wranglers convincing him to hurry along. Tonight, there was only Liberty. And Kenny, if he ever finished saddling up.

The kid drove a hard bargain. His assistance was going to cost Liberty four pieces of her mother's leftover fried chicken and some homemade pineapple coleslaw. She'd conceded without a fight. Deacon needed a hazer, and Kenny was their only available option.

"Come on, you mangy beast. Quit your dawdling."

Shouting and clapping her hands, she moved the steer the last few feet into the chute.

Liberty hopped the fence and secured the spring-loaded door. That task completed, she fastened the barrier rope around the steer's neck—a sometimes tricky task that, thankfully, went easy tonight. Next, she readied the second rope, which would be strung across the box once Deacon was positioned inside it. When the steer broke from the chute, the barrier rope would snap off and release the rope barricading the box. Only then could Deacon spur his horse into action and begin the chase.

Hearing the sound of hooves on hard-packed dirt, she looked up. Deacon approached the arena on Huck, his bay gelding. Smart choice, Liberty thought. Of his two horses, Huck was also her pick.

"Ready?" she called to him.

"As I'll ever be."

If he doubted his abilities, he didn't show it. Deacon sat tall in the saddle as he confidently guided the horse into the box. Once in position, he looked up, and their glances locked. Neither of them spoke.

The next instant, Kenny rounded the corner of the barn on one of the Becketts' ranch horses. He nudged the lanky gray into a fast trot, his big smile revealing the sizable gap between his two front teeth.

"I can already taste that chicken," he said as he lined up his horse on the opposite side of the chute.

"Sure you don't need a practice run?" Liberty asked Deacon, willing to consider it if he said yes.

He shook his head. "Got the timer?"

She pulled the electronic device from her pocket. Before going after the steer, she'd located a spare timer in the office. Normally, contestant runs were tracked by an electronic clock in the announcer's booth. They were going old-school tonight.

Holding the timer high for Deacon to see, she placed her other hand on the chute lever and readied herself.

He took another minute to adjust his seat in the saddle, check the reins and shove his hat farther down onto his head.

Liberty considered taking out her phone and capturing the image with her camera. This was the Deacon she liked most. The man who was all cowboy without a trace of lawyer. Because he'd no doubt wonder why she was taking his picture, she settled for committing the image to memory.

An emotion, and the revelation that came with it, swept swiftly through her, leaving her slightly unbalanced. She didn't just like Deacon. Wasn't simply attracted to him. Her feelings were far more complex…and deeper.

She'd only just righted herself and replaced her hand

on the lever when Deacon gave the "go" signal by nodding curtly.

Heart pounding a mile a minute, Liberty pulled the lever. With a bang, the chute door opened and the steer bolted for the open arena. Kenny and the gray set off at a gallop, running parallel to the steer and keeping him in a straight line.

An instant later, the barrier rope broke, and Deacon was out of the box, already leaning forward in the saddle, his left foot leaving the stirrup in preparation. Huck's hooves dug into the arena floor like giant shovels, spraying clumps of dirt in their wake.

It took only a second for Deacon to catch up with the steer. Dropping the reins, he launched himself out of the saddle and, in one spectacularly fluid motion, dropped onto the ground, grabbing the steer's horns as he landed. The heels of his boots plowed into the dirt, at first losing then gaining traction. His shoulders bunched, and the fabric of his shirt pulled tight around the thick muscles of his upper arms.

Liberty glanced at the timer and sucked in a sharp breath. "Come on," she urged in a low voice. "You can do it."

Cranking his arms counterclockwise, Deacon attempted to drop the steer to the ground. It resisted, equally determined to break free. Deacon didn't give up. Another powerful thrust, and the steer's knees buckled. The next instant, it lay on the ground, and Liberty stopped the timer.

"You did it!" She gave a loud whoop and jumped down from the fence, so excited she almost forgot to check the time. She did then and stared for several seconds at the numbers.

Deacon climbed to his feet and retrieved his hat. Still out of breath, he stood bent at the waist, his hands braced on his thighs.

"Good run, cowboy," Kenny said, trotting back to Deacon and leading Huck behind him.

Timing aside, it had been a good run. Liberty was pleased for Deacon and proud of him. His technique might be a little rusty, but he hadn't lost it.

Grunting with indignation, the steer hoisted himself upright and loped off, glad to be done with the whole distasteful affair. Kenny went after him, leaving Huck behind. The gelding gave a lusty snort of satisfaction, then stood quietly.

Liberty ran to meet up with Deacon, her speed impeded by the soft dirt. She reached him just as he straightened to his full, impressive height. Bulldogging was considered a big man's event because of the strength it required, and Deacon fit the bill perfectly.

Without thinking, she threw herself at him. "You did it!"

He caught her as they collided, his grip strong and possessive. "Yeah?"

"See." She showed him the timer. "Eight-point-seven seconds."

"Not great."

"Not bad, either, for a guy who hasn't bulldogged in a while."

"I'll get better." He pulled her closer until scant inches separated them.

Liberty's heart cartwheeled. This was nice. More than nice, it was…sweet heaven! Her insides melted as his brown eyes bored into hers.

"Does that mean you're getting back into rodeoing?" she asked, unable to look away.

"It means I'm going to give practicing with the guys a try. See how it goes. I still like team penning." The pressure of his hands increased. "With you."

Mild warning bells went off in Liberty's head. Really? Now? She sighed. This probably wasn't a good idea. Not under the circumstances. She should extract herself from his embrace or at least say something.

She didn't utter a word. Not about their proximity or the sizzling tension it generated.

"You were amazing tonight. And your technique is good."

"My technique, maybe, but I'm a little out of shape." He rolled his right shoulder, wincing as he did. "I might have pulled a muscle."

"Ice it when you get home."

His gaze, already dark to begin with, smoldered. "I could try some stretching exercises."

"Stretching exercises?"

"Like this."

He wrapped his not-so-afflicted-after-all arm around her waist and hauled her solidly against him. A tingle of awareness spread slowly through her.

They had never stood so close. She had only to lift her mouth to his and magic would surely happen. His palm pressed into the small of her back, and because it felt natural to do so, Liberty slid her one free hand up to his shoulder.

Too bad she was still holding the pesky electronic timer. If not, she could use both hands. She considered dropping it, but that would probably be too obvious. Or would it? Her grip loosened.

"You don't have to help me clear my name if you don't want," he said.

Had she misread his signals? Did he not want to kiss her?

"A bet's a bet," she answered a little dejectedly.

"And I'll help you, too. With Mercer and your mother."

"Seriously?" That cheered her.

"It's my job to make my client happy if I can, and reconciling with your mom will make Mercer happy."

"Thank you, thank you!" Without thinking, she laid her

cheek on his chest and hugged him hard. With only one arm. She was still holding the stupid timer.

It was wonderful. Deacon, all rock-hard muscles and impressive height, made her feel soft and small and utterly feminine. He hugged her back, too, pressing his lips to the top of her head.

Friendly, chaste and as far as things should probably go. Liberty didn't know much about attorney ethics. Kissing her surely violated one or two of them even if she had thrown herself at him.

What if someone saw them? Kenny hadn't gone home yet. She should stop this now. For Deacon's sake. But when she tried to pull away, he held her fast.

"Not yet," he said, and dipped his head.

Liberty promptly dropped the timer. It fell with a muffled thud onto the dirt at her feet.

The kiss was everything she'd dreamed of these past two months, and her imagination had run pretty wild. His lips moved tenderly and expertly over hers with just the right amount of pressure to weaken her knees. Even as he encouraged her lips to part, she was already surrendering, willing him to take what she gave with tiny, needy sounds.

He must know what he was doing. She couldn't be this susceptible to a mere kiss. This affected. This aroused. With each passing second, Deacon grew bolder. She did, too, and he liked it, if she correctly interpreted his body's response.

Which was why his sudden ending of the kiss and setting her aside surprised her. Just when things were getting good, too.

"I may have overstepped my boundaries," he apologized in a voice as unsteady as Liberty's legs felt.

"Obviously, I didn't mind."

He retrieved the electronic timer from where she'd

dropped it and placed it in her hand. "We shouldn't let this happen again."

"I'm hoping you'll reconsider."

"Liberty."

"Okay, okay." She didn't want him to ruin the moment. It was, however, too late. "You don't have to explain. Things are complicated. You're Mercer's attorney."

"Yeah." He sounded disappointed.

Well, so was she. "But it won't always be that way. And when it isn't…" She smiled hopefully. "We can always try this again."

He brushed her cheek with the pad of his thumb. "There isn't anything I want more."

A thrill wound through her. She wasn't alone in her feelings. "I'll be waiting."

"No promises when that might be."

"I won't compromise your relationship with Mercer."

"I think it's me who's compromising you."

If only.

Deacon walked over to where Huck stood patiently gnawing on his bit and grabbed the reins. "If you wait until I've put him up, I'll drop you off at the house."

"That might not be such a good idea." Alone in the cab of his truck, they'd no doubt engage in a repeat of the past few minutes.

"I suppose you're right."

At the arena gate, she hesitated at the post and flipped three switches, turning off the floodlights. "See you tomorrow, Deacon."

"Night, Liberty." He tugged on the brim of his cowboy hat before striding purposefully toward the barn, Huck following.

She'd keep her word, she thought as she headed to the house. She wouldn't cross any lines or make trouble for him with Mercer.

It would be difficult, though. Not that Liberty had been kissed by *that* many guys, but Deacon was by far the best. Working with him on the arena operations and team penning would be a challenge.

She couldn't wait.

Chapter Seven

Deacon checked off another name on his list as he hung up the phone. Today alone, he'd attempted to reach seven former Easy Money employees. Three of the numbers had resulted in dead ends. The four individuals he'd managed to connect with weren't much help. They were glad to hear from him, pleased—and surprised—to learn he was an attorney, but had nothing of value to contribute regarding the day of Ernie's accident.

They'd *seen* nothing, *heard* nothing, and even if they had, they *weren't saying.* Just like the three wise monkeys.

Deacon had come to the conclusion it was time to take the bull by the horns, no pun intended. Walter wasn't the only person still around who'd been at the arena the day of the accident. Sunny had been there, too.

Placing a quick call, he asked if she was available to meet with him. During the conversation, he casually confirmed Liberty's whereabouts. She was with a student's family, looking at a horse for possible purchase. Much as he wanted to see Liberty, it was better he didn't today. Not until he'd spoken with her mother.

He and Liberty had been doing their level best these past three days to maintain a strictly professional relationship. The kiss they'd shared, incredible as it had been, was a mistake they couldn't repeat. Not while he represented Mercer.

Thoughts rolled around inside Deacon's head as he drove from his office to the Easy Money. He was close to finalizing the partnership agreement and had only a few years' worth of financial reports left to review. They were also waiting on the real estate appraisal, the title search and most recent property tax assessment.

In the meantime, a routine was slowly developing among the Becketts. Though they didn't always agree, Sunny and Mercer worked well together and had two more bucking contracts to show for their efforts. Liberty and Mercer, too, were amicable. On the surface anyway. Deacon suspected that for the sake of her family she'd set aside her hurt and frustration at being lied to.

Cassidy bristled whenever she was near Mercer. She had, however, grudgingly allowed her son and Mercer to spend supervised time together—an arrangement that pleased Mercer enormously. He'd taken quite a shine to his young grandson. Benjamin also liked his newfound grandparent. Mercer was the first person he sought out when his mother brought him to the arena.

The front office was empty when Deacon entered. He didn't think much of it. Tatum's hours varied, depending on the needs of her three children. Sunny was good to her office manager. She'd been good to Deacon once, too.

"Hello," he called out, and started for Sunny's office.

"In here."

He was surprised, and not surprised, to find Cassidy seated in the visitor chair. Bringing reinforcements was typical for the Beckett women.

"How are you doing today?" He purposefully kept his voice neutral so as not to put her on the alert.

"Fine." She rubbed her forehead. "The air-conditioning up and died last night. We're waiting on the repairman. I might have to duck out if he calls."

"I won't take long."

Sunny wasn't making excuses. Both she and her daughter looked tired and sported dark circles beneath their eyes. No air-conditioning in the heat of summer could ruin a person's sleep.

"The title company emailed me a preliminary copy of the title report this morning." She lifted a slim stack of papers from her desk.

Deacon leaned against the same file cabinet he had before. He supposed he could follow Mercer's initiative and fetch a chair from the outer office. For reasons hard to explain, he didn't.

"This isn't about the partnership agreement."

"No?" Sunny leaned forward.

"Then why are you here?" Cassidy asked.

"I want to discuss the accident." Though he probably didn't need to clarify, he did anyway. "When Ernie Tuckerman was gored."

Sunny spoke slowly and thoughtfully. "Your involvement in that accident has no effect on my opinion of you as an attorney. I'm sure you're a good one."

"I know I'm a good one. And I wasn't involved in the accident, other than being here when it happened and taking the blame."

"Why does it matter now? No one cares or even remembers."

"It matters to me, and people do remember." If they didn't, he'd have more clients on his roster.

"For the record," Sunny said, "I didn't believe you were responsible."

"Then why let me take the fall?" Anger rose inside him, potent as the day of the accident when Sunny came to him and intimated it was his fault.

"Not intentionally responsible."

"Your job was to take care of the bulls," Cassidy interjected. "And you were the last one seen at the pens before they escaped."

He went over to the rack on the wall where the keys hung and flicked the nearest one. "The office door is left open during business hours. Anyone could have taken the key to the pen."

"That's true," Sunny concurred. "But who would do that and why unlock the gates? It makes no sense."

"Right. More likely a stupid, foolish kid was forgetful."

"I *never* thought you were stupid, Deacon."

"You looked no further. Ernie accused me, and that was all it took."

"He wasn't the only one."

Deacon remembered the taunts and the shame they accusations had caused. "Really? Did people really blame me or just go along with the general consensus?"

Sunny's demeanor cooled. "The insurance investigator determined the incident to be an accident. You weren't cited in any of the reports."

"I expected more from you, Sunny. Hoped for more." There, in a nutshell, was what haunted Deacon, now and for these past eleven years. "You were kinder to me than my own mother. I thought, of all people, you would stand behind me."

Her resolve visibly wavered. "I was under a lot of pressure, which, I realize, is no excuse."

"You fired me."

"Something I regret."

"Easy to say that now."

"I had to protect the arena. My reputation. My family. After you left—"

"I ran away. There was no reason to stay."

"It made you look guilty," Cassidy said, her tone less forceful than earlier.

"Very convenient for you." Deacon addressed his words to Sunny.

"You're right," she admitted. "I could have handled the situation differently. Better."

That was an understatement. "How do you look yourself in the mirror each morning? All the lies you've told to Liberty and Mercer, all the situations you didn't handle well. Are you okay with that?"

Deacon's intentions hadn't been to confront Sunny, only to find answers. But her easy dismissal of her past wrongs annoyed him.

Cassidy jumped to her feet. "You have no right to talk to my mother like that."

Sunny also stood. Very straight. "He does. I've made my share of mistakes. All I can do at this point is apologize."

"You should know I'm doing my own investigation."

"How can I help?" Her offer appeared genuine.

After a moment of indecision, Deacon accepted it and found his anger abating. "Answer my questions. You can also spread the word. Tell people you don't think I left the gates open. See if that sparks any interesting responses."

"Are you sure? You may not like what you find out."

"If the accident was my fault, if I inadvertently did something I don't remember, I need to know." He pushed off the file cabinet. "Now, if you'll excuse me…"

With that, he left. The walls were closing in on him, making it difficult to breathe.

He should go home, he thought, stopping at the bottom of the porch steps. The small Santa Fe–style house he'd purchased a mile from town was his pride and joy. Except Deacon craved wide-open space and a way to blow off some steam.

In the arena, participants were starting to gather for the evening's team penning competition. He'd been too busy to enjoy his favorite pastime since Mercer retained him.

Tonight, for a change, he was free. His mind was further made up when he spotted Liberty leading her saddled mare from the barn. She must have returned while he was in the office with her mother.

Striding toward her, he met her in the middle of the open area.

"Hey." Her smile was warm and welcoming.

Letting his gaze travel to the arena and back to her, he asked, "Looking for a partner?"

LIBERTY SAT ASTRIDE her horse, waiting for their turn. Three teams were ahead of hers and Deacon's, but with only sixty seconds on the clock to separate three calves from a herd of thirty and drive them to the pen at the other side of the arena, team penning was a fast sport. They wouldn't have long to wait.

Ricky Lopez had joined her and Deacon. Ricky was an old acquaintance of her mother and Mercer's and had lived in Reckless his entire life. He was also the person whose stories about her parents had finally prompted Liberty to contact Mercer.

"Okay if I go first?" Deacon asked. He sat beside her on Confetti. Another good choice. The mare was further along in her training than his gelding and possessed a natural instinct for calves.

"Sure. If Ricky doesn't care."

The other man nodded. "I'll take turnback."

There were different strategies in team penning. Sometimes, the three riders each assumed responsibility for one calf. Liberty, Deacon and Ricky had team penned together before and found a different strategy worked best for them. The first man or woman would return for the third calf, leaving the other riders in charge of the first two calves.

Liberty didn't mind that Deacon had asked to be first.

Insisted, really. She'd sensed something amiss with him from the moment he'd asked to be her partner.

Though curious, she'd refrained from inquiring. She had no right. They weren't friends—friends didn't kiss like they couldn't get enough of each other—and they weren't really business associates. Besides, this was neither the time nor the place. She and Deacon, not to mention Ricky, took their team penning seriously. If they intended to walk away in one of the money spots, they needed to concentrate. Also, study the herd.

Each of the thirty calves had a number affixed to their rump. Three wore zeros, three wore ones, three wore twos, up to nine. A number was randomly drawn when the riders entered the arena and announced after the flag was raised, signaling the start of their time. Until then, the riders didn't know which three calves to cut from the herd.

Noting unique identifying marks helped. Anything to shave seconds off the team's time. One number seven had a crooked ear. One number nine sported a white patch on its left shoulder. The black two and brown four constantly hugged the fence.

If her team drew any of those numbers, she'd point the calf out to Deacon. While he went after it, she'd locate a second calf with the same number and be ready for her turn.

A lot of strategy. When it came to team penning, some said calf-smart was more important than horse-smart. Liberty thought it was a combination of both.

The announcer's voice blared from the overhead speakers. "Thirty seconds remaining." With only one calf cut from the herd, the team currently competing had better hurry.

Their last-ditch efforts, though admirable, fell short. They ended the allotted sixty seconds with only two calves in the pen and officially out of the running.

"Team one-oh-four." Cassidy's voice blared from a bullhorn. "One-oh-four. You're on deck." She exchanged the bullhorn for a two-way radio and spoke into it. Part of her job during penning competitions was to maintain constant contact with the announcer's booth, which happened to be manned tonight by their parents.

Funny, Mercer wasn't with the livestock. That was typically the livestock manager's job. Not that Walter wasn't more than qualified to handle it. But Mercer had said he wanted to learn the ropes.

Apparently being with his ex-wife took precedence. More than ever, Liberty was convinced her mother was receptive to the idea of reconciling with Mercer. Already this week they'd conferred with a contractor regarding repairs to the barn and arena and traveled to Tucson to check out a stud horse for potential breeding—all part of Mercer's goal to expand the bucking operation.

Questions continued to haunt Liberty. She believed her mother would be more willing to answer them if she was on better terms with Mercer. Anger at him was what had motivated her lies in the first place.

"Ready?" Deacon asked when Cassidy called their team on deck.

"Let's do this." Ricky nudged his horse forward.

The team currently competing was performing well. Their time would be the one to beat. Liberty studied Deacon rather than the calves. The furrows creasing his brow looked less like concentration and more like anger.

What had happened today? She'd seen him coming out of the office right before he joined her. Had he met with her mother or researched more records? Liberty had gotten busy immediately after that and forgotten about it up till now. Maybe she should have paid closer attention. Especially if they wanted to win tonight. Distractions were costly.

Speaking of which…she promptly took her own advice

and got into the zone. As an employee of the arena, she didn't share in any winnings. If her team placed, her portion of the proceeds went to a fund that sponsored youth riders.

Donating her share didn't lessen her desire to win.

Okay, Mercer was right. She *was* a little like him in that she'd inherited his competitive nature. Just like her brother and sister.

One of the wranglers swung open the gate. It was their cue to enter the arena. Riding three abreast, they started down the length of the arena at a slow, steady walk. The pen stood to their right. A row of panels hooked together created a barrier to aid in driving the calves into the pen.

At the midway point, a flag was raised and the announcer called, "Number two, number two."

Deacon and Liberty broke into a trot. Ricky stayed behind, his job to keep the rest of the calves away from the pen and the number two calf—once collected—in close proximity. "Eleven o'clock," Deacon called, giving the location of the first calf.

"Four o'clock," Liberty responded, pinpointing a second one.

Almost immediately, the number two calves bunched up behind their buddies and hugged the wall. This was not going to be easy. Liberty relied on her mount's natural abilities. The gelding moved as if an extension of her body, responding to the slightest pressure from her legs or hands.

Deacon pulled on his reins and veered left. The small huddle of startled calves sprang apart. Number two made a dash for freedom. With heart-stopping accuracy and skill, Deacon cut the calf from the rest and drove it along the arena fence to Ricky. The crowd in the bleachers cheered. Regardless of whom they were there to support, they respected good technique when they saw it.

It was Liberty's turn next. She kept her number two calf in constant sight while also watching Deacon. Relaxing her hands, she let the gelding do his job, correcting him only when necessary.

The calf zigzagged. Liberty and her horse stayed on him. At the exact right moment, she separated the calf from the herd and headed it down the arena. More applause sounded from the bleachers.

Only one calf remained. Deacon was already in motion. In less time than before, the calf was loping toward the others. Ricky rounded them up, holding them near the pen until Liberty and Deacon arrived. All three riders had to push the calves into the pen for the run to qualify.

The buzzer went off, and Liberty's glance traveled to the board. An instant later, their time appeared, along with their ranking. Second place. Not bad.

"Bueno, mis amigos." Ricky raised his hand for a high five.

She returned it enthusiastically, then said to Deacon, "We make good partners."

His reply was to ride ahead.

"Something the matter with him?" Ricky asked as they exited the arena through the gate.

Across the way, the team waiting to go next discussed last-minute strategy.

"Not sure," Liberty said, intending to find out. Catching up with Deacon at his truck, she demanded, "What the heck's wrong with you?"

He hauled the saddle and blanket off his horse and stowed them in the truck bed. The bridle came next.

"Don't you even care how we did?" Talking to him from atop her horse was stupid. She swung down and, doing precisely what she'd warned her nephew not to, dropped the reins. "We're in second place."

Brush in hand, he stopped just short of running her over. "You can give my share of the winnings to the youth riders, too."

"What's bothering you? Tell me," she insisted when he began vigorously brushing his horse.

"Nothing I can talk about with you."

"Because it involves my family," she guessed.

He moved to the horse's other side.

"My mother," she concluded, thinking Deacon wouldn't have gotten this upset with Mercer.

"And your sister."

Ah. That explained a lot. "Those two can upset anyone."

He didn't concur, just continued grooming his horse.

Nice hands, Liberty thought. Large and strong and well shaped. She'd touched them. The back of one to be specific. And she'd felt them gripping her arms and waist when they'd kissed.

What would it be like to hold one between her own hands, their fingers linked as they walked side by side? In some ways, that would be more intimate even than kissing.

"I asked her some questions about the accident."

So much for contemplating hand holding.

Her gelding took a few steps toward Deacon's mare, his nose extended for a sniff. Liberty didn't care as long as they played nice. No nipping or kicking.

"What did she say?"

Deacon threw the brush in the truck bed. "That she also didn't think I left the gate open."

"Then why are you angry?"

"She still let me take the fall. Said she had to protect your family and the arena."

Liberty sighed. "My mother's like that. Willing to hurt one person if, in her mind, it protects another. Heck, she lied to me my entire life. For my own good, according to her," she added with a bitterness she felt to her core. As much as she loved her mother and tried to understand why she'd done what she had, Liberty still struggled with forgiving her. "I realize that's no consolation."

Deacon untied the mare's lead rope with a hard yank. "I need to walk her out."

"I'll go with you." She stooped to retrieve her horse's reins. Luckily, the gelding had behaved himself. Otherwise, she'd have a lot of explaining to do.

She and Deacon didn't talk during their first circuit behind the barn. Eventually, he broke the silence.

"I placed a lot of calls today to former Easy Money employees and got nowhere."

That accounted for his mood.

"Talking to people is a good idea." She gave him a pointed look. "You just didn't pick the right one."

"I've already asked Walter," Deacon said. "He doesn't remember much about the accident."

"Not him." Liberty paused and waited for his gaze to meet hers. "Ernie Tuckerman."

To his credit, Deacon didn't react. "I told you already, he won't see me."

"How do you know?"

They stopped at the tack room, where Liberty tethered her horse to the hitching rail.

"Our last conversation wasn't pleasant," Deacon said. "I visited him in the hospital the day after the accident."

"What happened?"

"He accused me. I called him a liar. And a name or two I won't repeat in the company of a lady."

"We all say things we regret when we're mad. He may not hold a grudge against you."

"When's the last time *you* talked to him?"

"Actually, he comes to the arena now and then. He's always nice to us."

"Because he doesn't blame you for what happened."

"Talk to him," Liberty urged. "He's the only one who saw the entire accident."

She would have bet money on Deacon refusing. Apparently he wasn't as easy to read as she thought.

"Fine."

"Really? When?"

"Saturday. I'm tied up with work until then."

Beaming broadly, Liberty said, "Great! Make it in the afternoon, and I'll go with you!"

Chapter Eight

Deacon had completely lost it.

What other explanation could there be for letting Liberty accompany him to Ernie Tuckerman's sorry-looking single-wide trailer in a run-down RV park? It had been her idea, and he wouldn't be doing it without her insisting. Still, he should have come alone.

Ernie might feel less threatened with only one person questioning him. Questioning, Deacon reminded himself, not confronting. Then again, Ernie might be more comfortable with someone he knew and, according to Liberty, was nice to.

"Did your mom ever talk to Ernie about the accident?" Deacon asked.

Liberty turned away from the passenger window to answer him. "She was in on the interviews with the insurance investigator."

"Did Ernie cooperate?"

"He must have. He blamed—" She stopped short.

"Me."

Great. All signs pointed to this adventure going awry big-time.

Deacon parked on the side of a dirt road traversing the center of the RV park. There was only one tiny space beside each trailer. Ernie's was occupied by an older model ready-for-the-junkyard sedan.

"Whoever said Reckless doesn't have a wrong side of the tracks is mistaken," he commented.

Liberty opened her door. "This place wasn't always such a trash heap. The previous owner kept it kind of nice. He died, and his wife hasn't been able to manage things on her own."

"Too bad. It's a decent location. Has she ever considered selling?"

"I don't know her well. Mom does. Her husband used to serve on the school board with Mom."

The address numbers attached to the side of Ernie's trailer hung crookedly. Crisscrossing tears had left a star-shaped hole in the lower half of the screen door. Years of exposure to the sun had faded the original tan color of the trailer to a bland white. Deacon didn't let himself think about what the inside looked like.

On the stoop, he rang the doorbell. No chime sounded in return.

"Try knocking," Liberty suggested.

He did. Instantly, the deep bark of large dog sounded from inside the trailer. A few moments later, the door rattled as a series of locks was undone. The excessive security was probably completely unnecessary. All anyone wanting inside had to do was pry open one of the flimsy windows.

The door continued to rattle, and the dog's barking increased. Deacon's gut clenched. He hadn't told Liberty on the ride over how nervous he was about meeting Ernie, but, unless she was completely self-absorbed or incredibly insensitive, she'd probably guessed as much.

Her suggestion to talk to Ernie was a good one. He'd thought of it before. Several times since his return. But he'd always dismissed the idea.

Because he was afraid.

As much as Deacon believed he'd shut the gate on the bulls' pen, a very small part of him allowed for the possibility he had forgotten. Finding out the accident really was his fault scared him.

"Remember," he warned Liberty in a low voice, "I do all the talking."

"Sure, sure," she whispered.

He wasn't buying it.

The trailer door suddenly opened, accompanied by a whoosh of air from the evaporative cooler mounted in the window. Ernie stood there, staring at them through the screen door and holding a huge Rottweiler by a chain collar. The barest flicker in his expression was all that gave away his alarm at seeing them.

"I'm busy," he said over the sound of the barking dog. "What do you want?"

"To talk," Deacon coaxed, employing his best attorney demeanor. "If you have a few minutes."

"About what?"

"Can we come inside?"

"No. I got company."

If he did, the company was staying out of sight. Or couldn't be heard over the dog. Deacon thought the excuse was more likely fabricated. Nonetheless, he respected the man's wishes.

"I could come back later," he suggested. "At a more convenient time. Or meet you in town. Buy you a beer at the Hole in the Wall."

That stirred a reaction in Ernie. It was quickly followed by a vehement head shake. "Can't. Car's not running."

"He can pick you up," Liberty interjected.

Deacon silenced her with a warning glance.

"I'm not going anywhere with you." Ernie's gaze narrowed as his voice rose. "I'm not going with you until you tell me what you want."

The dog lunged at the torn screen door. He'd have come through the hole if Ernie didn't have a firm hold on his collar.

Liberty flinched.

Deacon instinctively put himself between her and the dog. "I see now how the screen was damaged."

"Leave it, Samson," Ernie commanded. "And be quiet." As if a switch had been flipped, the dog instantly sat and stopped barking. Twisting his giant head around, he licked the part of Ernie's arms he could reach. "Good boy."

Deacon was impressed. Maybe Ernie wasn't such a bad guy after all. He had suffered a grave injury that left him partially disabled. That would turn anyone into an ill-tempered recluse.

With the dog subdued, Deacon moved closer to the door. "I want to discuss the accident."

Something flashed in Ernie's dark eyes. With the screen between them and partially obscuring Deacon's view, it was hard to determine what. Anger? Resentment? Hatred?

Possibly. In addition to his physical injuries, Ernie probably suffered from post-traumatic stress disorder. It was common in people who'd survived serious injury, and Deacon bringing up the past could have triggered a reaction. Without professional counseling, and with lingering injuries, Ernie might still be struggling to cope.

He'd been a handsome young man, though it was hard to tell that today. And talented. Too bad he'd also been cocky and overconfident. He'd been one of Deacon's tormentors. The worst, in fact, often egging his pals on to greater heights.

Funny how their lives had changed. Deacon ventured a guess that neither of them had ever figured this was where they'd be eleven years later.

"What about the accident?" Ernie demanded.

"I'm trying to piece together what happened."

He visibly tensed. "Why?"

Deacon debated his answer, then settled on the truth. "I believe someone other than me left that gate open. May have even intentionally sabotaged the gate to get back at me."

"Why would they do that?"

"That's what I'm trying to find out. Another possibility is they were targeting you."

"Me!" He rocked unsteadily on his bad leg.

"I thought if we sat and talked, had a beer, you might remember more about the day of the accident."

"I remember all I need to. I was standing by the bull pen when all of a sudden, Heavy Metal came charging through the gate and ran over me like I was an empty pop can in the road. I didn't stand a chance."

Liberty pushed her way closer to the door. "Why were you standing by the bull pen?"

Ernie glowered at her and swore under his breath. Samson, apparently sensing a threat, started a low rumble from deep in his throat.

She didn't take the hint. "Practice was over. The bulls were bedded down for the night. There was no reason for you to be there."

"Liberty." Deacon hooked her by the elbow and eased her back. "I'll ask the questions."

"Ask away." Ernie dragged Samson from the door. "I'm not answering any of them."

"Look, Ernie—"

"Get off my place. Now, or I'm calling the sheriff and having you arrested for trespassing."

The next sound was that of the trailer door slamming in Deacon's face. For a moment, he didn't move.

"Oops." Liberty grimaced guiltily. "Guess I blew that."

"You think?"

"He didn't have to be so rude."

Deacon didn't wait for her. His patience had worn too thin.

"Hey, not so fast." She scurried after him. "It was a good question."

He didn't respond until he was seated behind the steering wheel and inserting the key in the ignition. "It was a great question."

One he hadn't thought of. And he called himself an attorney.

Why had Ernie been at the bulls' pen? There could have been any number of good reasons. He'd forgotten a piece of equipment. One of the bulls had been acting strange, and he went over to investigate. Instead of explaining, Ernie had gotten angry and thrown Deacon and Liberty off his place.

Something wasn't right. "He knows more than he's saying," Deacon concluded.

"You think?" she mimicked him.

"Save the sarcasm, will you?"

"That's what I get for helping." She slumped against the seat, her bottom lip protruding.

He drove no more than a hundred feet, then hit the brakes and threw the truck into Park.

"Something wrong?" Liberty asked.

Deacon let the truck idle. "What was the full extent of Ernie's injuries?" He'd left a few days after the accident. Ernie was still in the hospital, recovering.

"Shattered leg. Broken ribs." Liberty stared thoughtfully out the window as if remembering. "One of the ribs pierced his lung. A ruptured spleen. The doctors removed that. A whole bunch of internal injuries. The worst was the infection. He nearly died. They had to go in and remove part of his lower intestine. He wears one of those bags." She patted her side.

"A colostomy bag."

"Yeah, that."

Deacon had assisted on a case during his internship. That client also wore a colostomy bag as the result of an accident and, thanks to the law firm employing Deacon, he'd received a substantial settlement from Social Security for retroactive disability payments.

"Do you know how Ernie gets by? Money-wise."

"Not really. I assume he receives some kind of government assistance."

"Not much, obviously, or he wouldn't be living in a trailer." Deacon rubbed his chin, the wheels in his head turning. "Did he receive a settlement from your mother's insurance company?"

"Oh, I'm sure he did."

"Do you recall how much?"

She shook her head. "Mom would know."

"Can you ask her? Without raising too much suspicion."

"I can try. But why?"

Rather than answer her, Deacon took out his cell phone and placed a call to his friend and boss at the law firm where he'd interned. "Murry, it's Deacon McCrea. Good, good. How are you? No, I'm in Reckless. Opened my own practice." After a few more pleasantries, he got to the point. "I could use your advice on a potential case. It has to do with going after the Social Security Administration for back disability payments. That's right. The guy has a colostomy bag."

Beside him, Liberty sat up straight, her wide eyes fastened on him.

"You're a nice guy, Deacon. You didn't have to do that."

"He deserves more than he's obviously getting."

"He was rude," Liberty insisted. "Most people wouldn't repay that with kindness."

They were almost to the arena after their encounter with Ernie Tuckerman. Nothing special was scheduled for tonight and there was no reason for Liberty to hurry back. With a dust storm in the weather forecast, few people, if any, would show up for practice.

Ideal circumstances for spending more time with Deacon. Only she couldn't, she thought glumly. He still represented Mercer, which quashed their chances for a relationship. But she'd seen a different side to him this afternoon. A most appealing side that fueled her attraction to him.

He had every reason to dislike Ernie Tuckerman. The man had single-handedly driven Deacon from town. Tarnished his name. All but thrown Deacon off his place. Yet, the first thing Deacon had done upon leaving was to call a former associate and see if there was some way he could help Ernie.

What was wrong with her? She should have asked Deacon out on a date when he first returned instead of waiting for him to do the asking. Then maybe he wouldn't have taken Mercer on as a client.

Live and learn. They would simply have to wait until all the legal stuff between her parents was finished. More reason than ever for her to try to orchestrate a reconciliation between them.

"I feel guilty," Deacon said.

Was he kidding? "About Ernie?"

He sent her a glance. "What if I did leave the gate open?"

"You didn't."

"I didn't mean to."

This was new and a little alarming. "Are you doubting yourself?"

"I remember locking the gates."

"There. See?"

"What if I didn't secure the latch or fully engage the padlocks?"

"Both sets?" She made a face. "Impossible."

In his position, it would be hard not to doubt himself. "If you did leave the gates unlocked, then what happened was truly an accident."

"Yeah." He didn't sound convinced.

She decided to change the subject for the last five minutes of their ride. "Have you made any progress with getting Mercer and Mom together?"

"I suggested they meet privately to discuss the final partnership agreement. Without attorneys and without family members."

"I like it, but what if they argue over the terms?"

"Oh, you can count on that."

"Then what's the point?"

"Don't worry. They'll meet in the middle. They have to in order to continue running the Easy Money. Your mother isn't about to let it go under. And if they can meet in the middle over business…"

"They can meet in the middle about other things," she finished for him.

"What about you and Mercer? Have you resolved things yet?"

"No." She drummed her fingers on the armrest. "He's invited me to talk a couple of times. I've put him off."

"That might speed the process. If your mother sees that you and Mercer are making an effort, she'll be more receptive."

Liberty chuckled mirthlessly. "I haven't resolved things with her, either."

"It's tough dealing with parents."

"I'm not the only one having trouble," she added pointedly.

His jaw visibly tightened. "I don't have to work side by side with both of mine, for which I'm very grateful."

"Have you seen your dad at all since you got back?"

"The other day. Briefly. I had an appointment in Phoenix

and stopped in Globe on the way home to drop something off for Mom. He was there for a change."

That was progress. Last she knew, he'd been avoiding his father.

"How'd it go?"

"We didn't sit down with a beer and watch the game together."

"Maybe you will. Eventually."

"I can't wait," he answered drily.

Another change in topic might be called for. "Have you tried contacting any more former employees?"

"I've about exhausted my list."

"Still no luck?"

"I was thinking of contacting former customers that might have been around the day of the accident. You don't by chance remember any?"

"I remember our customers. Not if they were at the arena when the bulls got loose. Sorry." And she was. "I can ask Mom."

"If you're going to ask her anything, I'd rather know the settlement amount from the insurance company."

The Easy Money entrance came into sight. "Where do you want to be dropped off?" he asked as they turned into the driveway.

"The house. I have laundry to do and dinner to fix. It's my turn to cook tonight."

"Ah, the glamorous life of a riding instructor and endurance horse trainer."

"Don't remind me."

She enjoyed the easy camaraderie they shared and consoled herself with the fact they could be friends, if not romantic partners. It was better than nothing. But, truthfully, she wanted a whole lot more than nothing.

He parked in front of the closed garage door and got out of the truck.

"You don't have to see me in," she said.

"When I take a lady out, I walk her to her door."

Out? This wasn't a date, though parts of it had reminded her of a date. The conversation, the driving, the relaxed moments of silence in between the talking.

"Well, thank you."

Liberty went to a small panel mounted beside the garage door and lifted the cover. No sooner did she enter in the code than the door lifted in a noisy chorus of grinding and scraping.

Heat from inside the garage blasted them. It was like standing too close to a roaring bonfire.

Deacon raised his arms in front of his face as if to shield himself. "Next time we use the front door."

Would there be a next time? Liberty sensibly reminded herself this was no date and their kiss the other day had been a one-time spontaneity.

"Gotta love these Arizona summers." She entered the garage, Deacon on her heels. Her mother's Chevy sedan was gone. Liberty remembered that Cassidy had driven Sunny to Globe for an eye doctor appointment. The house would be empty.

A wall of shelves covered the entire left side of the garage. Like most people, the Becketts had filled theirs with holiday decorations, old suitcases, miscellaneous camping equipment from days gone by and what Liberty referred to as mystery boxes.

"Don't look." She held her hands to the sides of her face to create blinders. "It's all Mom's stuff, I swear."

"You should see my garage."

"How bad can it be? You only just bought the house, what? A couple of months ago."

"You'd be surprised." He stopped suddenly and stared at the ceiling.

"What's wrong?"

He pointed to the access door. "Does that lead to your attic?"

"Yeah, why?"

"Tatum mentioned you have some old records stored there."

"What are you thinking?"

"That I'd like to have a look at them. Would your mother mind?"

"You need them for drawing up the partnership agreement?"

"Technically, no."

"That's our story," she said with a mischievous smile. "And we're sticking to it."

She reached for the cord dangling from the access door and pulled. It opened to reveal a rickety attic ladder folded in on itself.

"I don't want you to get in trouble," Deacon said. He stood behind her, gazing into the dark hole above them.

"I'll handle Mom."

He helped her unfold the ladder. The bottom step exactly reached the floor. Placing her foot on it, she grabbed the railing and started up.

"Spot me." As she ascended, Deacon held the sides of the ladder so it wouldn't wobble. Liberty moved slowly. It was like crawling into a cave. A sweltering cave.

"Can you see up there?" Deacon asked.

"There's a light." Reaching the top, she waved her hand back and forth in front of her. "At least, there was one." Finally, she felt the pull string brush her wrist. "Got it." A quick tug, and the attic was bathed in the feeble glow of a forty-watt bulb.

My, my, when had they acquired such an incredible array of junk?

"What exactly are you searching for?" She glanced down

to find him staring back at her. Her breath caught and not because she was inhaling 140-degree air.

He'd taken off his cowboy hat. She tried to recall a time she'd seen him without it. Not often and not lately. His sandy-brown hair defied its obvious recent trimming and curled attractively at the ends. It looked soft to the touch. If only she could test her theory.

"Client records," he said. "From the time of the accident."

With some effort, Liberty tore her gaze away from Deacon and scanned the attic interior. Perspiration dripped into her eyes, clouding her vision. Wiping at it with the back of her hand was useless. Fifteen seconds up here, and already she was on the verge of succumbing to heat stroke. Whatever records Deacon needed, she'd best locate them fast.

A tower of file boxes loomed straight ahead. Someone had written "Customer Contracts" and a corresponding year on the outside with a thick black marker. Considering how organized her mother was, they could hold only one thing.

Liberty quickly identified the two boxes she'd need. Kneeling in front of the tower, she yanked the first one free. The tower tipped precariously. Miraculously, she managed to stabilize it before being buried in an avalanche. Setting the box on the floor, she went after the second one.

"Can you get these?" She pushed the boxes across the attic floor to the edge of the opening.

Deacon climbed halfway up the ladder and, retrieving the boxes one at a time, carried them down.

"You sure those are the right years?" She wasn't about to climb down only to have to go up again.

He lifted the lids and quickly inspected the contents. "Perfect."

Liberty took stock of her situation before easing into place and picking her way blindly down the ladder.

"Need any help?" he asked.

Good grief, he was close. She was acutely aware that her backside hovered inches above his face. Embarrassment caused her to momentarily lose her footing.

"I've got you." He placed his hands on her hips and steadied her.

Could this get any worse?

"I'm okay. Really," she insisted, but he didn't remove his hands. Not until she was standing on solid ground.

"Are you all right?" He studied her with concern. "You're bright red."

"It's hot up there."

Surely the heat had something to do with her flushed state. It couldn't all be from her butt waving in the air.

"I really appreciate it." He smiled. A killer smile that caused her breath to catch. Again.

"No problem."

"I owe you."

There was a change in his voice. It became softer. Silkier. The kind of voice a man used when he murmured against a woman's bare skin.

"I'll collect one of these days." She tried to be flippant. Casual. Instead, she practically purred.

"Anytime." He brushed away a strand of hair that had become plastered to her cheek.

Thinking she must look awful, she averted her head. Besides being hot, the attic was filthy.

"Come here." Deacon's hand slid up and circled her neck, drawing her closer. There was no mistaking the hunger in his eyes.

"I thought we agreed. No kissing."

"That was before you did me a favor."

An entirely different kind of heat invaded Liberty, this one from the inside out. It turned her bones into jelly and drained the last remnants of her willpower.

He dipped his head until their lips barely brushed. She could almost taste him. Wanted to taste him. Needed to.

"Deacon…"

"Mmm?" His warm breath caressed her, tempting her further.

"You're killing me."

"Aren't you exaggerating just a little?"

It didn't feel like it.

The next instant, he claimed her mouth and saved her from what would have surely been a terrible fate.

She arched into him, desperately seeking contact with every long, muscular inch of him. He obliged her by fusing their bodies together. A moan escaped her. His mouth, his tongue, what he did to her should be illegal. It felt that amazing.

One kiss melted into two. Three. More. There was no stopping. All that mattered was him. Them. This incredible sensation she didn't think she could live without. When he turned her in his arms, she tightened her hold, afraid he was going to end the kiss and shatter her dreams. Thank you, thank you, she thought when he promptly picked up where he'd left off.

The sound of spitting gravel and a vehicle pulling into the driveway halted them with the same suddenness as being drenched with a bucket of cold water. They broke apart to discover Sunny and Cassidy staring at them from the front seat of the car with matching startled expressions.

In that moment, the boxes of contracts they'd smuggled from the attic were the least of Liberty's concerns.

Chapter Nine

"I appreciate you talking to me, Joe." Deacon cradled the phone between his neck and ear while jotting notes on a piece of paper.

"Just wish I could've been more help," the man on the other end of the line said. "I always did think it was strange that Ernie went over to the bull pen when he told everyone he was going home. And that electric shocker I found on the ground. I knew the Becketts didn't condone the use of them."

In the two years Deacon worked at the arena, the use of electronic shocking devices had been strictly forbidden. Some cowboys and handlers believed that giving bulls a zap before releasing them from the chute made for a better ride. The Becketts didn't subscribe to any practice remotely hinting of animal mistreatment.

"What did Sunny say when you told her?"

"Never brought it up," Joe continued. "Seemed wrong, what with Ernie getting all busted up like he did and almost dying."

Deacon pondered this development. As an attorney, he deemed the discovery of an electric shocker to be important and relevant. Sunny and the insurance investigator should have been told. Saying something now would make no difference. And there were those—Ernie, for one—who might say Deacon had used the shocker on the bull.

Deacon decided to file the information away for the time being.

"On the contrary," he told Joe. "You've been a big help. And I'm looking forward to seeing you at the Helldorado Rodeo next week."

"Wouldn't miss it. I'm interested in checking out the operation now that Mercer's back in charge."

"I think you'll be pleasantly surprised."

"Him and Sunny sure did wonders with that place. Barely more than kids themselves when they bought it." Regret tinged his voice. "For a hundred years, the Easy Money was the best rodeo arena in the state. Then it was sold and sold again. Mismanaged and misused until it was no more than a pile of timbers. Sunny and Mercer, those two had the touch. Turned the arena completely around in just a few years. While raising two youngsters of their own to boot. A real shame when his dad died. Heart attack out of the blue, they say. These things happen, but Mercer, he couldn't deal with his grief and took to the bottle."

"Yes, sir." Deacon didn't interrupt Joe's recollections. He owed the livestock agent that much in exchange for the information he'd supplied about the electric shocker.

Joe Blackwood had been at the arena the day of the accident to inspect the bucking stock for his employer, a rodeo organization out of Tucson, and negotiate a new contract. A big fan of the sport himself, Joe had stuck around to watch the young cowboys practice their bull riding for the upcoming state finals. He'd been, and still was, familiar with anyone making a name for themselves.

He'd been watching Deacon and Ernie in particular, as two of the arena's most promising competitors, and seen Ernie head over to the bull pen shortly after Deacon finished feeding and locked up. Unfortunately, he hadn't noticed anyone tampering with the gate locks.

Deacon had been placing calls to Easy Money clients since getting his hands on the boxes of old customer contracts. Though he was having better results than with the former employees, he still didn't have enough hard-core evidence to make a case. Either there was a conspiracy underfoot to protect someone—which Deacon highly doubted—or only two people had been at the bull pen that evening: Ernie and Deacon.

He had Liberty to thank for the files. They'd kept Deacon busy during his downtime, which was a good thing as his mind tended to wander lately, always in one direction.

Kissing her the first time could be chalked up to an impulsive mistake. The second time in her garage, there was no excuse. Deacon had allowed his desire for her to overrule his common sense and had been lucky Sunny hadn't run straight to Mercer.

In fact, she and Cassidy had said nothing about the kiss. After a rather awkward moment, Liberty explained that they'd retrieved the boxes from the attic for Deacon and that was that. The three women went inside and Deacon left for his office.

He'd avoided the Easy Money as much as possible this past week, going only twice to exercise his horses at times when he knew the Becketts would be occupied. He and Liberty had talked by phone. She'd told him she hadn't received any flack from her mother about the kiss. Cassidy had teased her in the way sisters do, but that was all. Deacon wasn't sure what to think. Were Sunny and Cassidy in favor of his involvement with Liberty? He found that hard to believe, especially Sunny, considering how their last meeting had ended.

"Congratulations again on your new practice," Joe said,

returning Deacon to the present. "Who'da figured you for an attorney. No offense intended."

"None taken, sir." Deacon had received that same reaction so often in recent months that his skin had grown as thick as an elephant's hide. "Talk to you again soon."

Moments after he disconnected, Deacon's part-time secretary Anna Maria poked her head into his office. She was young and inexperienced but made up for it with eagerness and dedication. Eventually, if all went well, he'd hire her on full-time. A legal assistant, too. That was, if Mercer didn't get wind of Deacon's ethics violation and make trouble for him.

Could he be more stupid? By kissing Liberty he'd not only put himself in a compromising position but her, as well.

"Mr. Beckett's here to see you," Anna Maria said, the hint of a Mexican accent giving her voice a pleasing lilt.

Deacon immediately rose, and his glance darted to the contract boxes on the floor beside his desk. "He's not due for another twenty minutes."

"I can tell him you're busy and to come back later or wait."

"It's all right. Give me two minutes, then show him in." Apparently Mercer was taking a page out of Deacon's book.

"No problem," she said, and disappeared.

Deacon used the time to store the contract boxes out of sight.

"Hey, Mercer." Deacon stood to greet his client. They shook hands across his desk.

Mercer immediately made himself comfortable, grabbing a bottled water from the small refrigerator in the corner before sitting. He'd initiated the meeting, making the appointment with Anna Maria and not giving any specifics.

Deacon couldn't help noticing that the other man's customary grin was missing. Sunny must have told him about the kiss. Was that the reason for his visit?

"How are things?" Deacon strived to remain cool. No point anticipating trouble.

"Great. That's what I came by to tell you. Entries for the Helldorado Rodeo are at a record high."

Deacon recalled his conversation with Joe. "That could be because of you. People in the rodeo world are glad to have you back at the Easy Money. And the bulls you're leasing from the Lost Dutchman Rodeo Company are the best in the area."

Mercer made a sound of disgust. "That's what I wanted to talk to you about."

"Okay." Not Liberty and lines that shouldn't be crossed. "What's wrong?"

"I'd like it a lot better if we were using Easy Money's own bulls."

"You still thinking of purchasing some with your own money?"

They'd discussed Mercer's wish to expand the arena's bucking stock operation before. He was determined to include bulls. Deacon supported him. To be truly a top bucking stock contractor, the Becketts couldn't limit themselves to horses, steers and calves.

"Sunny's dead set against it. We talked again this morning."

That must account for Mercer's lack of a smile. "I thought you two were getting along."

"Like peas in a pod most days. That notion you had about the two of us finalizing and signing the partnership without anyone else there, it was a damned good one."

Deacon agreed. Good for his client and also good for Liberty's wish to reconcile her parents.

"She's softening toward me, I can tell," Mercer continued. "Except where those bulls are concerned. A buddy of mine called me yesterday with a lead on six potential champions for sale. If I don't bite, someone else will."

"Give her a little more time to get used to the idea," Deacon suggested.

"That's what Liberty said."

Interesting. "You two are talking then?"

"More or less."

"I'd say she's softening toward you, too."

Mercer's grin finally made an appearance. "You think?"

"She wants you in her life." Deacon hadn't done very well with his own parents. The McCreas were and would always be a dysfunctional family. Liberty and the Becketts, however, were different. They had a real chance at normalcy.

"She has a lot to forgive—to both me and her mother."

"Then it's up to the two of you to give her a reason to do that."

"You're a sharp one, Deacon."

"That's debatable." Kissing Liberty came immediately to mind.

"No, it's a fact. Folks were wrong to accuse you of causing that accident with Ernie."

"I appreciate the vote of confidence."

"I hope you figure out what really happened that day."

"It was a long time ago."

A glint flashed in his eyes. "Heard you've been asking questions."

Deacon shouldn't be surprised. News traveled fast, and he'd been contacting a lot of people.

"I'll stop if you feel it's interfering with my work for you."

"Stop? Hell, I'm offering to help you if there's anything I can do."

Did he mean it? One way to find out.

"The insurance company sent a representative to investigate the accident. There was a report."

"You'd like a copy?"

"I realize I'm asking a lot."

Mercer nodded thoughtfully. "I'll see what I can do."

"Thank you." Deacon felt only a small stab of guilt. He didn't deserve Mercer's kindness, not after kissing the man's daughter. Repeatedly.

"About those bulls for sale." Mercer returned to the reason for his visit. "Is there a loophole in that partnership agreement?"

They discussed the terms of the agreement and Mercer's ability to contribute assets to the Easy Money without Sunny's consent.

"You're walking a fine line," Deacon said when they were done. "She could sue you for breach of contract."

"I'm willing to risk it." Mercer rose. "I need to get back to the arena. A bunch of officials are coming out from the school district this afternoon. You know Sunny's on the board."

"I remember."

"She and Liberty are teaming up with the school to offer riding classes. Kids will earn some kind of extra credit. No money for us. But we get to take a tax write-off and, as Sunny points out, it's good for the community."

"That'll keep Liberty busy."

"She thinks the program will bring in new business."

"She could be right."

"I've been doing my share this week. Landed two more new customers. A rodeo out of San Antonio and another one from my old stomping ground in Kingman."

"That's encouraging, Mercer."

"Better if we had bulls."

"Be patient." Deacon escorted Mercer to his office door. He reached out and gave Deacon's shoulder an affectionate squeeze. "I've been spreading the word around town what a good attorney you are. You should be getting a referral or two in the near future."

"Thank you, Mercer."

"If things keep going the way they are with Sunny, I may not need you anymore. Hope you don't mind."

"I understand."

Frankly, Deacon couldn't be happier to lose a client. Then, there'd be no conflict of interest, and he'd be free to date Liberty.

"Instead of working for me," Mercer announced happily, "you can work for the Easy Money."

"Sunny already has an attorney in Globe."

Mercer dismissed the matter with a wave. "You're local."

Deacon had clearly gotten ahead of himself. He could no more date Liberty with the Easy Money as a client than he could while her father retained him.

Unless, of course, he refused the offer.

"I WANT PIZZA!" Benjy skipped down the sidewalk ahead of Cassidy.

"Come back here, young man," she called, and hastened her steps. "This instant!"

Liberty resisted rolling her eyes. Her sister and nephew had been doing pretty much the same thing for the past thirty minutes. Whose idea was it anyway to have dinner in town?

Oh, yeah. Hers. Their parents had driven to Apache Junction to meet with the Lost Dutchman Rodeo Company about bulls for the Helldorado Rodeo next week. Though not usually as well attended as the arena's other rodeos, it was an important one to those competitors attempting to qualify for the National Finals Rodeo and needing every possible win.

This year, entries were through the roof, some of them

from as far away as Oklahoma and Texas. Mercer was determined to secure the best bulls for the event, hence the trip to Apache Junction.

Of course, he'd rather they were using their own bulls, a point he drove home with anyone who would listen. Liberty was surprised her mother had agreed to go with him on the short excursion. Then again, she thought hopefully, maybe Sunny's desire to be with Mercer overrode her objections to owning bulls.

Liberty liked to think so. She'd been the one to suggest her mother accompany Mercer, and it hadn't required much convincing.

With the evening to themselves, the sisters had decided to eat out rather than in. Cassidy was already heading to town for Benjy's art class—both "art" and "class" being a stretch. Their office manager, Tatum, rented the empty space next to the Ship-With-Ease store and in her spare time gave group and private lessons to adults and children. She claimed it satisfied her need to teach until the school board voted in the new budget and hired her back.

Personally, Liberty thought her nephew was more the cowboy type than the artist type, but Cassidy insisted he be well-rounded. Her words. The once-afternoon-a-week Children's Introduction to Painting class had been a summer experiment. From all reports, Benjy cut up as much in the studio as he did in the arena.

After picking him up at Tatum's, the sisters stopped by the drugstore for a few necessities and were now deciding on a place for dinner. Liberty worried about not getting back to the arena. The long summer evening—one of the few remaining before school started—guaranteed a sizable crowd. But Walter was in charge during the Becketts' absence and could handle things for another hour.

"Are you sure you don't want tacos?" Cassidy asked.

She'd managed to halt Benjy seconds before he stepped off the curb by grabbing hold of his shirt collar.

"You promised pizza."

She had, Liberty mused with a smile. A deliberate bribe in the hopes of persuading him to behave during art class.

"Come on." She nodded at the light, which had changed from red to green. "Let's go."

It was a short walk to Tony's Pizza Parlor. Hopefully, Benjy would wind down by the time they got there. Cassidy had packed a few toys in her purse, just in case. Benjy didn't sit still unless he had something to keep him busy.

Reaching the other side of the street, Liberty glanced at the row of storefront offices, one of them Deacon's. Was he there now? He often worked late. His truck was nowhere to be seen, though that meant nothing. He always parked in the rear, leaving the spaces on the street for clients.

She knew this how? Because this wasn't the first time she'd checked out his place of work.

Great. She was a stalker. All right, not a stalker. But she did spend too much time thinking about Deacon. She'd spend less time if he'd come around the arena more or call her again. They were grown-ups. Surely they could handle being together without throwing themselves at each other.

She remembered their searing kiss in the garage and immediately dismissed that theory.

What if she talked to Mercer? Admitted she wanted to date his attorney. Right. Not happening. She and Deacon would just have to wait. The remaining loose ends of her parents' partnership agreement would soon be tied up. They *had* to be. Then Mercer would no longer require Deacon's services.

Tony's was packed as usual. In addition, the phone was ringing off the hook with pickup and delivery orders, adding to the chaos.

"What'll you have?" the waitress asked after delivering their sodas.

"Pepperoni and cheese." Benjy bounced in his seat.

"A large pepperoni and cheese," Cassidy clarified. "And a dinner salad on the side for me."

"Me, too," Liberty added. "With low-cal dressing." Pizza was her weakness. She told herself it was all right to have two small pieces if she didn't splurge on high-calorie dressing.

Such a lie.

"Anything else for the young man?" The waitress smiled engagingly.

"I hate vegetables." Benjy had constructed an obstacle course using his flatware, the salt-and-pepper shakers, a straw and sugar packets. Providing the sound effects, he drove his miniature race car through the course.

"That'll be all." Cassidy smiled apologetically at the waitress. "Thank you."

"Don't worry," Liberty assured her when they were alone. "This is a pizza parlor. Trust me, she's seen worse kids than Benjy. Probably in the last five minutes."

"Where's Grandpa?" Benjy demanded.

"With Grandma." Cassidy reached over and tenderly stroked his hair. "They'll be home later."

"Can he read to me tonight?"

Cassidy's hand stilled.

"Please," Benjy whined.

"I'll ask him. No promises."

Benjy returned to playing with his car, wearing a grin that resembled Mercer's. Cassidy wore a frown.

"He's good to Benjy," Liberty said.

"Can we talk about this later?"

"What did Mercer ever do to you?" Liberty asked in a low voice that was barely audible over the noise.

Cassidy sent her a sharp look. "Besides ruin my life?"

"Did he? Seems to me, we've always had it pretty good. Even without a father in the picture."

"You weren't there when he was—" she glanced at Benjy "—inebriated."

"Was he violent? Abusive?"

"No!"

"Because I heard he was mostly melancholy. He'd drink and start blubbering like a baby. He must have missed his father terribly."

"Look, I'm sorry Grandpa died, too. He was a great guy. We were all sad. That's no reason to throw away everything you have."

"Obviously, Mercer needed help. Support. Counseling. AA, whatever. Did he get it?"

Cassidy looked down at her place mat. "I don't remember."

"If you don't remember, then he probably didn't."

"What difference does it make?"

"Alcoholism is a disease. A person requires treatment to get better."

"I'm through discussing this," Cassidy hissed. "And I'm not going along with your absurd scheme to reconcile Mom and Dad, so don't ask me."

Liberty sighed. Cassidy refused to say whatever had happened between her and Mercer. Maybe that was something Liberty could talk to him about. A more comfortable starting point than his lying *to* and manipulation *of* her.

Tension lingered for the remainder of dinner. Liberty made several attempts to dispel it, then gave up. Cassidy was determined to remain a grump. There was one consolation. The pizza was warm and cheesy and oh-my-God delicious. Liberty forgot her earlier resolution and ate three pieces.

Leaving Tony's, they practically collided with Ernie Tuckerman and Tank Kluff, a lifelong local who worked as a maintenance repairman at the Roosevelt Mining Company in Globe. The two men appeared to have come out of the Hole in the Wall next door to the pizza parlor. The honky-tonk was actually nicer than its name implied and a popular spot for tourists.

"Howdy, folks." Tank patted Benjy on the head, then gave Liberty and Cassidy a smile. "How are you lovely ladies doing?"

Before either of them could reply, Ernie turned and, without a word, stormed off as fast as his bum leg would allow.

"What's with him?" Cassidy peered at Ernie's retreating back.

Liberty bit her tongue.

Tank gave an unconcerned shrug. "He's out of sorts. Apparently your visit the other day brought back a lot of bad memories from the accident."

"What visit?" Cassidy looked confused.

"Your sister and Deacon McCrea. They showed up at Ernie's trailer asking questions."

Cassidy whirled on Liberty. "You didn't think that was worth mentioning?"

"It was Deacon's business," she said, a touch too defensively. "Not mine to tell."

"And you're mad at Mom for keeping secrets." Cassidy grabbed Benjy's hand and tugged him down the sidewalk.

Liberty knew she should go after them, only she didn't. Frankly, she'd had her fill of her sister's moodiness. Enough was enough. They were all dealing with the fallout from Mercer's return. Liberty, too, and she managed to be agreeable. Most of the time.

"Sorry about that," Tank said. "Hope I didn't get you in trouble."

"It's all right. No worries."

"Me, I never had a problem with ole Deacon. But that Ernie, some things don't change."

This conversation had suddenly become more riveting. "He didn't like Deacon much?"

"Not then, not now."

"Because of the accident."

"Long before then." Luckily, the beer or two Tank had imbibed loosened his tongue. "It was no secret, he had it out for Deacon."

"Why?"

"Ernie was one talented bull rider, but if anyone could have beaten him, it was Deacon. Ernie didn't like that."

"Seems a little petty."

"To you. Not Ernie, not then. Rodeoing was all he had going for him in high school, and Deacon threatened that."

At the word "threatened," Liberty's suspicions rose. "What did Ernie do?"

"Took it upon himself after that to make Deacon's every waking moment a living hell. Teased the you-know-what out of him. Got everyone he could enlist to join him. It was Ernie who came up with the nickname Einstein."

She could believe that. No wonder he'd all but thrown her and Deacon off his place.

A thought promptly occurred to her. Did she dare ask it? What if Tank reported back to Ernie? She decided on a less direct approach.

"That's a lot of hate to direct at one person."

"It didn't stop with taunting. In my opinion, Ernie carried his grudge too far."

Her gaze narrowed. "What do you mean?"

Tank promptly flustered. "Wife says I talk too much for my own good."

"I don't think you're talking too much." She smiled winningly at him. "I'm enjoying your story."

"I'd better head home." He retreated a step.

Drat.

"Tell your folks I'll see them at the Helldorado Rodeo. We're taking the boy. It'll be his first one."

"Sure thing. Have a good night, Tank."

Liberty mulled over what Tank had said during her walk back to the truck.

In my opinion, Ernie carried his grudge too far.

Could *too far* be unlocking the gates to the bulls' pen and blaming it on Deacon?

That didn't make sense. Ernie was gravely injured in the accident. No one would risk their own safety simply to play a prank on someone. Or would they?

Regardless, she should tell Deacon. Right away. By the time she reached Cassidy and Benjy, she'd decided that if Deacon didn't come to the arena tomorrow, she'd go to his office. During the drive home, she decided not to wait that long and call him first thing.

Chapter Ten

As it turned out, Liberty didn't need to call Deacon. He was at the arena when she and Cassidy arrived. At least his truck was. According to Kenny, Deacon had headed off into the mountains an hour earlier. There were plenty of chores to keep her busy until he returned—which wasn't long after that. She paused while inspecting a students' new saddle, her gaze drawn to Deacon.

Riding his gelding, he trotted toward his truck. If he saw her, he gave no indication. She decided not to get mad or feel hurt at the slight. He could be preoccupied, as she was lately.

The horse was coated in a layer of dried sweat. Deacon must have ridden him hard. That was something Liberty did when she was bothered by a problem. An intense work-out could be good for both animal and rider.

Excusing herself from her student, she sought out Deacon. He finally looked at her when she was within a few feet.

"Hi, there."

"Hey." His smile didn't quite reach his eyes.

What did she expect? A warm embrace? Hardly. They'd agreed after being caught kissing by her mother and sister that there would be no public—and not so public—displays of affection. Not for the time being, at least. To assure that, Deacon had steered clear of her.

Liberty thought they were fairly safe standing in the open area between the barn and arena. Several dozen people milling nearby further insured they'd stick to the rules.

"Looks like you had quite a ride," she said, watching him unsaddle.

"I took the Aqua Vista Trail."

That accounted for the horse's sweat. The trail was notoriously steep and rugged, suitable only for advanced riders.

"I ran into Tank Kluff a little bit ago when Cassidy and I came out of the pizza parlor. He was with Ernie Tuckerman."

Deacon paused, then resumed removing Huck's saddle and bridle. But not before she caught a spark of interest in his dark eyes. "They've always been friends."

"Ernie took off the minute he saw us. But Tank hung around and talked for a while. He said something kind of interesting."

She had his attention now.

"What's that?"

"He told me about Ernie's grudge against you."

"*Grudge* is a strong word."

"Not according to Tank. In his opinion, Ernie took things too far."

Deacon finished brushing Huck and leaned against the truck bed, his arms crossed over his chest. "Go on."

"Actually, he clammed up after that." She reached out and touched his arm. "Deacon, I think Ernie may have opened the gate to the bulls' pen to eliminate you from the competition."

"Ernie knew better than to do anything so stupid as to let a bull loose."

"It makes sense in a weird way."

"Not to me."

"You're being obstinate."

The corners of his mouth quirked in amusement.

She was suddenly a little breathless.

"I spoke to Joe Blackwood last week," he said. "The livestock agent. He was there the day of the accident. Told me he found an electronic shocking device on the ground behind the bulls' pen."

"Oh! My God. That wasn't ours."

"They aren't hard to come by."

"You think someone shocked Heavy Metal?"

"Even if the gates were open, I still can't believe any of those bulls would charge. They were settled down for the night, fed and watered and bone tired after a long practice."

"Unless they were encouraged to charge," Liberty said. "With a shocker."

"If that's true, then Ernie was the target."

"But what about Tank's remark? That Ernie carried his grudge against you too far."

"Tank's either mistaken or talking about something else."

Liberty was less sure. Why else would Tank have left in such a hurry? "What are you going to do?" she asked.

"Nothing."

"Deacon! Someone used a shocker on Heavy Metal. Maybe some of the other bulls, too."

"We don't know that."

"Joe found the shocker on the ground."

"Circumstantial evidence at best."

"Come on!" Liberty couldn't believe how irritated she was at Deacon. Here were two valuable leads on what really happened the day of the accident, and he was ignoring them.

"My former associate got back to me." He gathered his horse's lead ropes and started walking.

Liberty fell into step beside him, still irritated but not ready to give up talking to him.

"He believes Ernie has a legitimate case to pursue back disability payments from the Social Security Admin. Ernie's retained him. I agreed to do the legwork pro bono."

She gaped at him. "You didn't?"

"It's the right thing."

And showed what a truly decent guy Deacon was.

"Does Ernie know?"

"That I referred my friend? Yeah."

"But not that you're doing the legwork for free?"

Deacon said nothing.

"Why not?" she insisted. "He should know. He accused you of something you didn't do."

"One doesn't have anything to do with the other. Ernie deserves the money that's rightfully owed him."

Liberty didn't care about the people who might be watching. She didn't care that she and Deacon had agreed there would be no more kissing. She flung herself at him and hugged him hard enough to knock him off balance.

It was quite satisfying.

BRAYING CALVES, BELLOWING bulls and whinnying horses made up only a fraction of the noise at the Helldorado Rodeo. There was also the constant blaring from the arena loudspeakers, the roar of the crowd and the rumble of trucks, trailers and cars coming and going in a nonstop stream.

Deacon had been to rodeos since leaving Reckless, usually attending three or four a year, however often his schedule allowed. Last year, he and a buddy had traveled to Vegas and spent three days at the National Finals Rodeo, just for kicks.

Always as a spectator. He hadn't competed since college, when he'd entered a few PCA rodeos. The competition at the professional level was intense, far exceeding the junior rodeo level. For any chance of placing, Deacon would have had to dedicate more time, energy and money than his studies permitted.

He'd loved college. Almost as much as he'd hated high school. Once his reading disability was diagnosed and Deacon was taught how to compensate, he couldn't get enough of learning. Strange how what started out as the worst thing to ever happen to him became the best.

Not that he'd ever brag about it. If anyone discovered he had a juvenile record, he'd lose clients right and left, and his career would tank. At least in Arizona.

"Hey, Deacon. How'ya doing?"

"Tank. Good to see you." He immediately recalled Liberty's conversation with Tank outside the pizza parlor. Maintaining a neutral expression, Deacon asked, "Who's this young cowboy?"

"My son. Jessie." Tank introduced the toddler he balanced against his broad chest.

"Nice to meet you, young man."

The boy studied Deacon warily, stuck his thumb in his mouth and turned away, more interested in the nearby catering van than Deacon.

Tank, once a stocky young man, had grown into his childhood moniker. *Literally* grown into it. "What are doing with that number stuck to your back?"

"Trying my hand at bulldogging."

"No joke! When's the last time you wrestled a steer?"

"Actually, just a couple weeks ago."

Tank's loud laugh came straight from his generous belly and startled his little boy. "Well, good luck to you," he said. "I'll be rooting from the stands."

The decision to compete in the Helldorado Rodeo might be something Deacon lived to regret. Despite what he'd told Liberty, he hadn't discounted her conversation with Tank about the electric shocker. It substantiated his suspicions of foul play. The perpetrator and the target, however, remained uncertain.

Deacon thought mingling with the cowboys at the rodeo, some of whom were around at the time of the accident, might be a way to gather information without drawing attention to himself. Also, people talked more freely with someone they considered one of their own.

Up till now, he hadn't learned anything useful. Up till now, he hadn't run into Tank Kluff.

One round of steer wrestling with Liberty wasn't enough practice. He was going to make a fool of himself. Well worth it if he learned something of value. So far, he'd struck out, but it was still early.

The Helldorado Rodeo was a two-day event, the preliminary rounds on Saturday and the finals on Sunday. They'd just resumed after an hour lunch break and would continue into the evening. Deacon had no hope of making it to the Sunday finals. He'd be happy enough to simply survive the steer wrestling.

"I'll need all the support I can get," he told Tank.

"Aren't you up next?"

"Soon." Deacon wasn't leaving. Tank had yet to say anything interesting.

"There's more of the old gang here today. You seen any of them?"

Old gang? Deacon had to suppress a bitter chuckle. He hadn't been part of Tank's or anyone's gang back in high school. But he cut the other man some slack. It was the least he owed Tank for giving him such a perfect opening.

"I've run into Vic and Hector and Woody." Deacon's glance traveled to the bleachers, overflowing with fans. "Is Ernie here? Liberty says he comes sometimes."

"No clue. I don't see him much. We're not close."

And yet they'd shared a beer the other day.

Deacon decided to be direct with Tank rather than indirect as he had with everyone else he'd spoken to today. "You were here the day of the accident. Do you remember anything that might shed light on what happened?"

A shadow flitted across Tank's broad face. "Other than you forgetting to lock the gate? I don't."

Funny. According to Liberty, Tank had said he believed Deacon was innocent. But here he was, practically accusing Deacon. Had he lied to Liberty or were Deacon's questions putting him on the defense?

"I didn't forget," Deacon said, any previous doubts vanishing. "And I'm beginning to wonder if you know something you're not telling."

"I wasn't there."

"You were. In fact, you were the first person to reach Ernie after Heavy Metal gored him."

"I meant I wasn't at the bulls' pen when Ernie got hurt. I didn't see anything, and as far as I'm concerned, we're through talking." His loud voice caused his son to start to whimper. Glaring at Deacon as if this was all his fault, he said, "You sure have changed."

The other man had no idea how much.

They parted with a terse goodbye. Deacon headed in the direction of the bucking chutes where he'd wait with the other cowboys, assessing the steer and the competition until their event started.

"Deacon?"

Hearing Liberty call his name, he wheeled and allowed himself a long, leisurely look at her. Damn, he'd missed her this past week. One brief encounter wasn't enough. It had required all his fortitude not to seek her out at the arena or phone her in the evening when the lights were low and the house was too quiet even for him.

She looked great. Slim-fitting Levi's accentuated her small waist and sexy curves. A pink checkered Western-cut shirt tucked neatly into the waistband and a tan cowboy hat perched on her head completed the outfit.

He swallowed, his throat suddenly dry. He'd held her by the waist last week when she hugged him, then let his arms slide around to her back. He hadn't wanted to let go. Ever. Staying away had been the only available option.

While Mercer had hinted at not needing Deacon's services in the near future, they hadn't officially terminated their representation agreement. Deacon could initiate it if he chose, and would as soon as it was feasible.

He drank in the sight of Liberty again. First thing Monday, he'd make an appointment with Mercer.

"I saw you and Tank over by the catering van," she said. "How did that go?"

"Fine until I brought up the accident."

She slanted him a look. "I don't suppose you posing a probing question or two had anything to do with that."

"Maybe."

She sighed expansively.

"You're right, Liberty. Tank's hiding something."

"Fat chance getting it out of him."

"Someone else will talk."

"Is that why you entered the steer-wrestling competition?" she asked.

"It gives me the chance to mingle without raising suspicion."

"You don't think Tank's suspicious?" Her teasing smile was contagious.

"I might have gone overboard."

"No." She feigned shock. "You?"

He laughed at that.

"I'll keep an ear to the ground, too. You competing in the steer wrestling is sure to get a few people talking. Especially when you eat dirt."

"You think I can't win?" He was mildly offended.

"You didn't do that great the other day."

"I didn't do that bad."

"You should have told me you were going to enter. I'd have signed you up for some practice sessions."

"It was last-minute." As in yesterday last-minute. "I'll catch up with you later, and we can compare notes."

"Promise."

"Sure." He started to leave. There wasn't much time left, and he still needed to ready his horse.

She gripped his arm, waylaying him. "Be careful today."

The warmth in her eyes and the tenderness in her voice compelled him to lean in closer. "Steer wrestling isn't half as dangerous as bull or bronc riding."

"I meant be careful you don't get somebody else mad at you with the questions you're asking."

She cared. And she wasn't mad at him for avoiding her recently.

As if to prove it, she stood on her tiptoes and planted a light peck on his cheek.

"For luck," she said. "I'll be watching you from the fence."

She turned and walked away, leaving Deacon standing there and most certainly wearing a dumbfounded expression on his face.

It was confirmed a moment later when Mercer sauntered over. "By the looks of you, I'd say you've been bitten hard."

"Liberty? She was wishing me luck."

"Mighty friendly way of wishing you luck."

"She's a friendly gal."

"That's what I've been hearing. By my count, this is the third time she's been friendly with you."

There was a bite to Mercer's tone. Someone—Deacon's money was on Sunny—had ratted on him and Liberty, and Mercer wasn't happy.

"I can assure you, there's nothing between Liberty and me."

"Didn't appear that way to me."

"You have no reason to worry. There's been no misconduct on my part. Either personally or professionally." He was stretching the truth. But there had been no intentional misconduct, and he and Liberty had stopped before things progressed too far.

"See that it stays that way."

"Yes, sir."

There was no mistaking the warning. Mercer didn't approve of Deacon seeing Liberty. He might not approve even after Deacon stopped representing him. Until he terminated their contract, Deacon needed to tread lightly.

At that moment, a voice blared from the loudspeakers announcing the start of the steer-wrestling competition and for all participants to report to the south gate. It couldn't have come soon enough.

He CAN'T POSSIBLY *WIN*. That was what Liberty told herself. Secretly, she hoped differently.

Deacon had steer-wrestled a total of once…in how many years? While he'd done passably well the other day, his time was nowhere near good enough to put him in the top. Not at this level of competition. Of the ten cowboys who had gone ahead of him, three finished in less than seven seconds.

Really, he didn't have a snowball's chance in hell. Still, Liberty watched from her place at the fence and chanted in a soft voice, "Come on, come on."

The chute door opened with a clang. The steer charged across the arena, kept in a straight line by the hazer riding beside him. The instant the barrier rope broke, Deacon spurred Huck into a gallop.

Liberty counted the seconds, matching them with the beating of her heart.

One...two...

Deacon caught up with the steer.

Three...four...

He flung himself from the saddle and onto the ground, his hands outstretched and ready to grab the horns. There! He had him.

Five...

His form was perfect. The steer turned his head, his legs going out from under him as if in slow motion. In that moment, she realized it was possible. Deacon could do this! He could place in the top four!

She cheered along with the audience, her fingers cramping from gripping the fence railing with all her might.

Then it happened. The unexpected. Deacon's feet suddenly lost their purchase. Instead of harmlessly laying the calf on its side, *he* went down like a sinking stone. The entire lower half of his body slipped beneath the rampaging steer.

He let go of the horns, unable to sustain his hold under the pressure. The steer stumbled as it trampled Deacon. Then, it was over. Deacon lay in the dirt, unmoving as the steer loped away. The buzzer cut the air, announcing his disqualification.

Liberty cried his name as the entire stands gasped in unison. She glanced frantically about, searching for the closest gate. Too far! Her foot hit the bottom rung of the fence, and she started to climb. Nothing was going to stop her from getting to him as fast as possible.

Then, something did stop her: the audience cheering. Pausing midstep, she looked up. Deacon was rising from where he'd fallen, putting first one foot and then the other on the ground. Standing at last, he waved to the crowd, signaling that he was unharmed.

The hazer rode over to him, having already herded Deacon's horse to the end of the arena where one of the wranglers collected him. The hazer spoke to Deacon, probably asking if he needed help. Deacon shook his head no and started back toward the chutes.

Liberty's knees betrayed her and she wobbled unsteadily. She clung to the fence, waiting for her strength to return. She'd seen countless falls through the years, some of those with tragic results. Yet, she'd never been more scared. And never been more glad to see a cowboy walk out of the arena under his own steam.

She raced to the exit gate beside the chutes, beating Deacon there. The instant he was through, she began fussing over him, mindless of the curious stares, bemused smiles and wolfish hoots.

"Are you okay?" She put her palm to his chest, then ran her hand down his arm. "Anything broken?"

"I'm fine."

"You're not." There was an angry red scrape on the side of his neck. "Maybe you should have the medic check you out." The entrant following Deacon finished his run. He must have done well judging by the crowd's enthusiastic response. Liberty hardly noticed. "You could have a broken rib."

"I didn't break anything." Deacon started walking away.

"Where are you going?"

"To get my horse."

She went with him over to the wrangler who held on to Huck.

"Better luck next time," the young man said from atop his horse.

"Thanks."

She hurried to keep up with Deacon as he led his horse away, matching her smaller steps to his longer ones. "You're not seriously going to try steer wrestling again," Liberty demanded.

"Not without more practice. I have three months before the Wild West Days Rodeo."

"Why? You only did this so you could mingle and ask questions."

"I had fun."

"Fun?" Liberty couldn't believe her ears.

He stopped at his truck to unsaddle the horse. "Isn't that why we do things? Because we enjoy them."

"Deacon." Emotion overwhelmed her. To her chagrin, she sniffed.

"What's wrong?"

"I thought you were hurt."

"I like that you're worried about me," he said gently.

She rushed to his side and buried her face in his shoulder. "You could have cracked your skull open. Don't do that again."

"So, is it my skull and not me you care about?"

His sexy voice sent a tingle dancing along her skin. "What do you think?"

She didn't hesitate, just stood on her tiptoes and kissed Deacon soundly. Right there in front of everyone. She didn't care who saw them or that they would probably be the talk of the rodeo before the night was over.

At first, he tensed. Then he returned the kiss. Only briefly but enough to ignite a warm glow inside her.

"Come with me tonight," he whispered in her ear.

"Where?"

"To the Hole in the Wall. Or the Flat Iron Restaurant. Both will be open late because of the rodeo."

"Are you asking me on a date?"

"We need to talk."

The warm glow dimmed. Until he smiled. How could she not have noticed the little creases that appeared at the corners of his eyes before?

A cowboy came up behind Deacon and clapped him on the back. "Good to see you competing."

"Thanks, Vic."

During Huck's cooldown walk, Deacon was stopped numerous times. It was a while before he and Liberty found themselves alone.

"Your father pretty much warned me to stay away from you."

"Because he's your client."

"I think more because he doesn't want to see you hurt."

'That's kind of…" Words failed her.

"Fatherly of him?"

"Yeah." Liberty took a moment to digest this new aspect of her relationship with Mercer. His actions were those of a doting father. Except a doting father didn't use his daughter like Mercer had used her.

Was she mad at him or touched? She wasn't sure.

"You okay?" Deacon asked.

"Sorry. I was just thinking about Mercer."

"We can skip tonight if you'd rather."

"Absolutely not." She refused to allow her issues with Mercer to affect her evening with Deacon. He might not think of it as a date, but she did. "There's a band playing the Hole in the Wall, and I want to go."

Music meant there would be dancing. She had no idea if Deacon even danced, but she intended to find out. The idea of him holding her close and swaying to a slow, easy number was just too tempting.

"We're going there to talk," he reminded Liberty.

"Sure, sure. I'll get away as soon as I can." She wondered who she could coerce into covering for her. "I have to go." She thought of kissing Deacon but was suddenly distracted. "I don't believe it."

"What?"

She pointed.

"Well, look at that," Deacon murmured.

Liberty's mother and Mercer stood in front of the door to the registration booth, locked in an embrace. A very passionate embrace.

"I was right," Liberty exclaimed. "Mom is still in love with him." She covered her mouth with her hand. "Cassidy's not going to like this."

"Don't tell her."

"She'll find out before the night's over. It's not as if they chose a dark, secluded corner."

"True. How do you feel about it?" Deacon asked.

"Mom's a grown woman. She can do what she pleases."

"Not that."

"I'm hopeful," Liberty admitted. "I can get past all the lies and secrets if my family's reconciled."

Deacon touched her cheek with the lightest of caresses.

Liberty swore she felt the ground sway. Then she realized it was just Deacon, sweeping her off her feet.

Chapter Eleven

The Hole in the Wall was about the worst place Deacon and Liberty could have picked for talking. Even when the band went on break, the noise level remained deafening. Deacon was all right with that—he'd rather dance with Liberty than talk. For now. They would have to get serious eventually.

He hadn't seen the place this busy before. The dance floor overflowed with two-steppers. Cowboys and cowgirls stood three deep at the bar and six or eight crowded around tables designed for four. Some were celebrating their wins at the Helldorado and advancement to the final rounds. Others were drowning their sorrows. Family, friends and spectators joined them.

Other than Liberty, none of the Becketts were there. They were probably still at the arena, taking care of last-minute preparations for tomorrow. Deacon should feel bad about stealing Liberty away, and he did. When they weren't dancing.

Then, he had trouble concentrating on anything except her. The delicate scent of her skin. The spark of laughter dancing in her eyes. The softness of her hand folded inside his. Her incredible curves that drove him to distraction.

"Deacon?"

"Mmm?" He looked down at her, mesmerized all over again.

"The music's stopped."

She was right. It had. "You ready for another wine?"

"Do you mind?"

She was drinking Chardonnay. Another contradiction he found fascinating. Not that white wine wasn't a lady's drink, but it wasn't much of a cowgirl's drink. Watching her sip from her long-stemmed glass while wearing jeans and boots and a leather belt was about the sexiest thing Deacon had ever seen.

He hoped she didn't notice how completely enamored he was with her. Then again, she'd have to be brain-dead not to. Even strangers smiled at them in a knowing way.

"Wait here." He left her at the edge of the dance floor and squeezed his way to the bar. Getting a waitress was impossible. With the room filled to capacity, the staff was being run ragged.

"Hey, Deacon." A pal and former junior rodeo rival stopped him. "Sorry about today."

"There's always next time."

He chatted with more old friends while waiting for the bartender to return with Liberty's wine.

"What about you?" the man asked, sliding the glass toward Deacon. He had the affable demeanor of someone who'd worked behind a bar many years.

Deacon produced enough bills to cover the drink and a tip. "I'm driving."

He had no desire to defend himself in court on DUI charges. Neither would he put a passenger of his in danger if he could help it.

Saying goodbye to his friends, he returned to where he'd left Liberty and drew up short. She was talking to Ernie Tuckerman and looking none too happy about it. Deacon walked briskly to cover the remaining distance separating them.

"Ernie," he said upon joining them, raising his voice to

be heard over the band. Handing Liberty her wine, he bent his head close to her ear. "You okay?"

"He was just asking me how the rodeo went," she said with exaggerated cheeriness.

"You should check it out for yourself tomorrow," Deacon suggested.

Ernie nodded. "I just might do that."

"Great." Liberty beamed. "I'll leave a guest pass for you at the booth."

His expression darkened. "I can pay. I don't need your charity."

"She was being nice." Deacon forced himself to remain calm.

"The Becketts are nice people."

Was he implying that Deacon wasn't?

Ernie raised his beer bottle to his mouth and took a long pull. "Heard you been asking questions around town about the accident."

Deacon felt no obligation to explain. "I'd still like to talk to you about it."

"I have nothing to say."

"Did you know an electric shocker was found on the ground by the bulls' pen right after the accident?"

"The Becketts don't allow shockers."

"Exactly," Liberty cut in. "Which is why it was strange to find one. And on the same day a bull escapes and charges you."

"You think I'd shock a bull just to get myself hurt? Nobody's that dumb." His gaze narrowed on Deacon. "Not even Einstein."

"Hey!" Liberty objected. "That's not very nice."

"Just joking with my old pal. He doesn't care, do you, Einstein?"

"I haven't cared for a lot of years," Deacon replied. "Not

since I graduated ASU in the top ten percent of my class and passed the bar on my first try."

"You did?" Liberty turned wide eyes on him. "I'm impressed."

"Yeah, good for you." The loud music didn't mask Ernie's malcontent.

The band finished their song and went right into another one without pausing.

"Liberty." Deacon reached for her hand. "Would you like to dance?"

"I think that's a good idea." She cast about for a place to temporarily set her wineglass. "There's Bill and Arlene. They're friends of Mom's. Just a sec." Hurrying over to the couple, she stayed a few moments to exchange pleasantries.

Ernie's gaze followed her. "I should've guessed you were tapping that keg when the two of you showed up on my doorstep."

Deacon loomed over him so that there would be no misunderstanding. "If I ever hear you say anything disparaging about Liberty or her family, I promise you'll regret it."

"You think you're so much better than me." Ernie shoved Deacon in the shoulder. "I have news for you, pal. You're nothing but a loser. Then and now."

"Watch what you're saying."

"You think you're smart. Like asking a lot of questions is going to make it look like you didn't leave the gates open. Everybody knows you did. And if they don't, I'm going to remind them."

"How dare you!" The voice belonged to Liberty.

Deacon and Ernie both turned to find her glaring at them.

"After all he's done for you," she said, "you should be thanking him. Not picking a fight."

"He hasn't done jack squat for me," Ernie spat out.

Deacon ignored the staring eyes and straining ears of nearby people.

"That attorney who's helping you with back disability payments?" Liberty said. "Deacon's doing all the legwork for free."

Instead of being grateful or contrite, Ernie growled, "I didn't ask for his help."

"Doesn't matter," Liberty insisted. "You're getting it."

"You can do better than him."

"I disagree." Liberty moved to stand next to Deacon.

Was Ernie interested in her? Deacon didn't think so. More likely his dislike of Deacon was responsible for his surliness. Nonetheless, Deacon wasn't taking any chances.

"Let's go." He grabbed hold of her hand and, without asking, led her out of the honky-tonk.

"Sorry," he said when they were outside. "Did you want your wine?"

Liberty made a sound of disgust. "He was unbelievably rude."

Deacon didn't release her hand as they crossed the parking lot to his truck. "Don't worry about it. He's angry."

"The accident was years ago. Time to move on."

"Easy for us to say. We don't walk with a permanent limp and wear a colostomy bag."

She stopped and, because their hands were still joined, she pulled him to a stop, too. "You're much too nice for your own good, Deacon."

"I feel bad for the guy. I know what it's like to have things rough."

"But you didn't let it turn you into a bitter semi-hermit."

"I could have. The only difference is someone helped me. When I didn't deserve it and didn't appreciate it. Not right away."

"Is that why you're helping Ernie?"

"I'm helping him so I can take a deduction on my income taxes for the hours I put in."

"Liar." She smiled. "You're paying it forward."

"Come on. It's late."

Opening his truck door, he helped her up onto the seat. As much as they'd touched tonight, at the arena and here, on the dance floor and off, it was starting to feel natural. And good. Really good. Deacon was going to hate for the evening to end, but end it must.

"Was there ever anything between you and Ernie?" he asked.

"Romantically? You can't be serious."

"He seemed protective of you."

"It's probably a carryover from Mom. She went out of her way to do things for him after the accident. She still does, once in a while."

"Like free passes to the rodeos?"

"He usually accepts. I think he refused only because of you."

It was a short drive to the Easy Money and the Becketts' house. The arena was empty and shut down for the night, the place in darkness except for security lights. They'd barely reached the driveway to the house when Liberty leaned forward in her seat, her jaw dropping. "I'll be damned."

"Something wrong?"

"That's Mercer's truck."

Deacon pulled in behind it, mindful of the barking ranch dogs that came out to greet them. "He's here?" It was more a question than a statement.

"I guess so." She nodded toward the road. "Let's go."

"You want to leave?"

"Yes." She said it as if he was missing the obvious. "I'm not interrupting them. They need to sort through their differences."

"*You* and Mercer need to sort through your differences, too," he reminded her.

"We will."

"You're stalling. Using your parents' reconciliation as an excuse not to deal with him."

She looked affronted. "I'm giving them some space. You saw them kissing earlier."

Deacon had to laugh. "How 'bout a coffee at the Flat Iron?"

"I'd rather go to your house."

He almost choked. "My house?"

"It's quieter," she said matter-of-factly. "We haven't had that talk yet."

Okay, she didn't mean what he'd first thought she did.

"Sure." He put the truck in Reverse, on edge despite her assurances that only conversation was in store for them.

During the short drive to his house, one thought kept running through Deacon's head. He hadn't ever been alone with Liberty. Really alone.

He trusted himself not to take advantage of the situation and her. Mercer was still his client and stood like a brick wall between them.

That didn't guarantee it would be easy for him. In fact, Deacon was convinced it would be anything but.

"MY FRIEND CHECKED the county court records. Ernie never sued your family or the insurance company."

"Why would he?" Liberty drank from the can of root beer Deacon had given her. He'd offered her something stronger, but two glasses of wine was her limit. Not that she'd finished the second glass. But it was getting late.

She probably should have let Deacon drop her off at home. But the thought of her parents together… It was too good of an opportunity to resist. Only later did she remember that Cassidy and Benjy were there.

Come to think of it, she was better off with Deacon. Cassidy wouldn't be happy about their parents and this latest development, and Liberty wasn't up for a lecture. She'd had too much fun dancing with Deacon.

He was right about her needing to sort things out with Mercer. She'd been avoiding any serious one-on-ones with him, convincing herself the reason was her conflicting feelings. Mercer being protective of her earlier today only further confused her.

"Why would Ernie sue us?" she asked. "He received a settlement from the insurance company."

"Not much of one."

"You're wrong." Last week, Liberty had wheedled the amount out of her mother. "It was a lot."

"It probably seems like a lot to you. But, actually, as far as settlements go for that kind of accident and one involving permanent injuries, it was on the low end of the scale."

She rubbed her thumb along the condensation collecting on the outside of her soda can. "Okay, the settlement was low-ish. Why does that matter?"

"Who takes less when they can easily have more? It's a red flag."

Deacon sipped from his own root beer. They sat on his couch in the family room. The entertainment center held a large flat-screen TV, currently off, and an audio system, currently on. Deacon, it turned out, had eclectic music tastes. They were listening to a soft jazz selection. His choice

Liberty had to admit she could grow to like jazz. More so if listening included sitting beside Deacon on this very comfy couch with its plush cushions.

The room was sparse in the way of bachelor men who weren't into decorating. It was also functional. The only real personal touch was a framed picture on the fireplace mantel, too far away for her to identify the people.

"Also, Ernie didn't retain an attorney after the accident."

Deacon had finished his soda in about three swallows, prompting Liberty to wonder what else he did fast. And what he did slow. Like kissing.

"And that's a red flag, too?" she asked.

"He was trampled and gored by a bull. Surely, someone advised him to seek legal representation. A family member. A friend. Heck, an ambulance chaser."

"Maybe Ernie doesn't trust attorneys." She sent him a pointed look.

"Are you insulting me?"

Because he'd been teasing, she teased him back. "I'm simply stating a fact. My mom hates dentists. Cassidy's convinced every salesperson is trying to rip her off. We all have people we don't fully trust."

"Who is it you don't trust?" He leaned closer. Enough that she could see those attractive lines in the corners of his eyes when he smiled.

"I'll tell you if you tell me what happened to you after you ran away."

He sat up straight. "We're getting off topic."

And like that, the door slammed shut. No matter how much she prodded, he wasn't going to share that era in his life. Which, naturally, made her all the more determined to find out what exactly had happened.

"Your family was liable," he continued. "But instead of suing, Ernie accepted the insurance company's initial settlement offer and signed a waiver."

"I still don't understand why you think that's important."

"It keeps coming back to an investigation. If he had sued, there would have been one."

"But there was," Liberty insisted.

"I mean there would have been a more thorough investigation. Both attorneys, his and the insurance company's, would have hired experts to comb every inch of the arena and interview every person there that day. The electric shocker Joe Blackwood found might have come to light."

"And you think Ernie didn't want that."

"He could have conceivably gotten millions."

"And instead, he spent his puny settlement in the first few years after the accident and lives in a single-wide trailer."

Deacon smiled approvingly. "You're starting to think like an attorney."

Liberty straightened. "Of everything you've said, everything you've uncovered, this makes me the most curious. He didn't retain an attorney for a lawsuit he almost certainly would have won. Mom should have asked these questions back when it happened. I'll tell you why she didn't," Liberty continued before Deacon had a chance to interject. "Because she was in a hurry to settle the claim and put the accident behind us. A lawsuit would have dragged on for months. Years, even. She's admitted she let you take the blame in order to protect the arena." Liberty sucked in a sharp breath. "Do you think she knows something she's not telling?"

"I doubt it. If I were in her shoes, I'd be relieved that Ernie didn't take me to court and not ask any questions. Why rock the boat?"

"I bet Joe's told someone about the shocker." Liberty considered potential candidates. "Like Tank."

"Or not. Joe has nothing at stake. Nothing to lose."

Deacon picked up his empty soda can and stood, groaning like an old, arthritic man rising from bed in the morning.

"Are you okay?" Liberty asked, instantly concerned.

"I might have pulled a muscle." He kneaded his right shoulder with his left hand.

"You probably pulled a lot of muscles. That was quite a spill you took."

"I think you're insulting me again."

"Do you have any ointment? I'll rub some into your shoulder."

At her remark, he went perfectly still. Something dark and dangerous flared in his eyes. "That's not a good idea."

"Hmm." She rather liked the idea of running her hands up and down his shoulder. He did, too, she'd wager, which might be why he'd refused her offer. "What about an ice pack? You need to do something. If not, you'll wake up tomorrow with ten times the pain you have now."

"There's ibuprofen in the medicine cabinet. Be right back." He left her sitting on the couch.

She sighed. Deacon was such a gentleman.

Maybe she should be less of a lady. Especially if she wanted him to—

Her glance drifted to the fireplace mantel and the framed photo. Deciding on a closer look, she pushed to her feet. The picture, obviously a candid shot, was of Deacon and another man who was definitely not his father and too young to be a grandfather.

The setting intrigued her. They sat side by side in metal folding chairs and were engaged in what was clearly an intense conversation. Deacon wore some sort of tan, baggy uniform.

"His name is Eduardo Frias." Deacon stood just inside the family room, watching her with an intensity that matched his expression in the photo.

"The mentor you mentioned?"

He nodded. "Eduardo was my detention officer."

"As in…"

"Juvenile detention."

Deacon had been in trouble. Serious trouble. She took a moment to absorb that.

"Sit down." He motioned to the couch.

"Is this a long story?"

"Not long as much as difficult to tell."

"You don't have to."

"I'd like your word it'll stay between us."

"Of course." She sat, tucking one leg beneath her. She'd been waiting weeks for this moment.

He dropped down beside her. When, after a few moments, he said nothing, she took his hand and squeezed it. That seemed to do the trick.

"I told you my leaving Reckless was spur-of-the-moment, and I didn't exaggerate. I hitched a ride to Phoenix and slept on the streets for about a week before I found my way to a homeless shelter."

"Deacon! How awful that must have been."

"Trust me when I tell you, it was hardly my low point. As soon as the shelter staff discovered I was underage, they called the police. I ran. Anything was better than being taken home."

She couldn't imagine the suffering he must have endured. Yet he'd chosen a life on the streets over the one at home.

Liberty liked to believe her mother would have taken Deacon's side if she'd known what would happen to him.

"I survived for the next two months. Barely. I did whatever I had to not to draw attention from the police, figuring if I could just hold on until I was eighteen, then I'd be legal. There's a big difference between a minor runaway and an adult missing person. But it was hot. Hot and dirty. I remember that the most. Going weeks without bathing. I'd sneak into public restrooms when I could and wash up in the sink."

"Where did you sleep?"

"Anywhere dry and shaded."

"How did you eat?"

"When I was really hungry, I stood on street corners with a cardboard sign and begged."

Liberty had always assumed most of those people were scammers, not genuinely in need. No more.

"I learned what churches had soup lines," Deacon went on. "Which convenience or liquor stores would trade food and water for a couple hours of sweeping floors and washing windows. I dived in Dumpsters."

"Oh, jeez, Deacon." Her hands flew to her cheeks. Tears pricked her eyes. "You didn't."

"I also stole. Small stuff. Food mostly. A radio. Batteries. Whatever fit in my pockets. Grocery stores were easier than convenience stores. Clerks there don't watch the customers as closely. Eventually, I was caught and became a bona fide member of the criminal system."

Liberty's chest hurt. It was, she realized, her heart breaking.

"Is that how you met Eduardo?"

"I was remanded to a juvenile detention facility in Mesa where I proceeded to make myself unpopular. Eduardo—Officer Frias—he took me under his wing. God only knows why. I gave him nothing but grief my first week there. It's because of him I was tested and my reading disability diagnosed. As the saying goes, it's never too late to learn. Reading opened up a whole new world for me. With Eduardo's help, I obtained my GED and enrolled in college. My grades were so poor I had to attend community college first. From there, I went to ASU."

"Did he encourage you to go into law?"

"Among other things."

"What else?"

"Return to Reckless. He's actually been to my office. It wasn't my office then. I was looking at spaces to rent, and he came along."

Liberty squeezed Deacon's hand harder. "He must be proud of you."

"That's what he says."

She couldn't be sure, but she thought Deacon's voice roughened just the tiniest bit, as if his emotions overwhelmed him. She was moved, by both his story and his obvious love for a man who was more of a father to him than his own.

Spurred by her own overwhelming emotions, she maneuvered closer to him. "If he comes to town again, I'd like to meet him."

"He'd like that, too. I've told him about you."

"Really?" A rush of pleasure warmed her. "What did you say?"

"Most recently, I told him I was sorry your father was my client. Otherwise, I'd ask you out."

More space between them vanished. Liberty's doing.

"My parents are getting back together. Mercer won't need you much longer."

"For which I'm very glad."

Liberty didn't wait for him to kiss her. She swung her leg over his middle and crawled onto his lap. Her hands came to rest on his shoulders with a soft sound of contentment.

"I could ask what you're doing." His gaze raked her face with a desire she hadn't ever seen radiating from a man's eyes.

It made her feel…bold. "Except you already know."

Dipping her head, she nuzzled his neck on the opposite side of his scrape. When her tongue darted out to taste his skin, he inhaled sharply. Liking the results of her efforts, she tried again in a different spot, right below his earlobe.

"You, ah, need to stop that."

She settled herself more snugly in his lap. "Is that what you really want?"

"What I want isn't what I should do."

My goodness, he was stronger willed than she'd given him credit for. "The partnership agreement's signed and sealed. My parents are reconciling. Mercer doesn't need you anymore."

"Liberty."

"One kiss." She pressed her lips lightly to his.

With a swiftness that threatened to unseat her, he threaded his fingers into her hair and molded her mouth to his. The sparks were instantaneous, and her surrender complete.

She wound her arms around his neck and pressed herself against him, as close as their positions would allow. No way could he mistake her meaning.

He didn't and groaned in ecstasy—or was it agony? Had she hurt his shoulder? He tightened his hold and angled her body, increasing the intimacy of their contact.

Nope, his shoulder was obviously just fine.

The kiss went on and on. She stopped caring about Mercer or proprieties or what they should and shouldn't do. Since that day in the garage, she'd been waiting for this. Dreaming of it.

Why, then, did Deacon abruptly pull away, leaving her breathless and a little confused?

"Is something wrong?"

"I promised your father there was nothing to worry about, that there were no improprieties between us."

"Can't you fire him or something?"

"I can terminate our representation contract."

"Then do it."

"I don't want you to get hurt."

"I'm a big girl, Deacon. I make my own decisions. About who I want to be with and what I want to do with them." Should he be uncertain, she traced the line of his jaw with her fingertip. "There are no guarantees. If I wind up hurt, or you for that matter, it will simply be a consequence of what happens. Not because one of us set out to hurt the other."

"I don't take this—us, what might be happening be-tween us—lightly."

"What *is* happening between us," she corrected.

"I care about you."

"If you didn't, I wouldn't be sitting on your lap, trying my utmost to seduce you. Frankly, I'm surprised you're re-sisting. I happen to think I'm irresistible."

"You are."

"Show me."

Hoisting her into his arms, he rose from the couch.

Liberty clung to him, then buried her face in his neck as he walked from the living room, down the hall and to his bedroom.

Deacon, perfect guy. Sweeping her off her feet yet again.

Chapter Twelve

"Make love to me, Deacon."

He'd been waiting for her to say that, anticipating this moment since he'd first seen Liberty a week after returning to Reckless. They shouldn't be here, lying across his king-size mattress with only one small light providing illumination. Not until he'd officially terminated his representation agreement with Mercer.

But she'd tempted him beyond reason, and Deacon had yielded. No one knew all the sordid details of his past, including Liberty. He'd told her more than anyone, however, and the connection he felt with her demolished the last of his defenses.

She was soft as silk. Everywhere. He knew because he'd been exploring her body's lush, slick places from the instant their clothes hit the floor.

The mild hum from the ceiling fan was the only sound in the room, save for the sexy, needy moans she emitted when she particularly liked where his mouth and fingers wandered. He might have groaned once or twice, a response completely beyond his control. The sight of her naked form in that shadowy half-light, her arms stretched over her head, was more than he could take.

"Don't stop," she pleaded, and pulled him onto her.

She was fire, and he the timber she consumed with a

mindless frenzy. No sooner had he settled his body along the length of hers than she lifted her hips to meet his. The contact set off a series of tiny explosions inside him.

"Are you sure?" He bit out the question between clenched teeth.

"What do you think?" She reached for the condom on the nightstand and tore it open with a playful grin.

He took it from her and quickly sheathed himself. No sooner did he finish than she took hold of his erection, the sensation nearly as exquisite as earlier when she'd teased and tortured him in ways that were permanently branded in his memory.

"Liberty, I—" His mind went blank as she guided him inside her warm folds. After that, he was lost. To her, in her, with her.

Slow, he reminded himself. He must go slow. Make this last.

"Deacon, please." She moved beneath him, rotating her hips and driving him wild.

"Yes." He increased his rhythm only marginally.

She dug her fingers into his buttocks, urging him on. Still, he didn't hurry, not until he felt the first tremors seize her. Then, he plunged into her, deep and fast.

She came quickly, like a spectacular fireworks display. His name fell from her lips over and over, ceasing only when their mouths were fused together in a searing kiss. Joined as intimately as possible for a man and woman to be, he shared the last moments of her release. Afterward, she lay limp beneath him, a serene, satisfied expression on her face.

"Mmm. That was…wonderful."

"Glad you enjoyed it." He nibbled the smooth hollow at the base of her neck.

She squirmed. "Stop it."

Ticklish. He'd have to remember that for later. And there would be a later. One night wasn't nearly enough.

"I can do better." He had yet to pull out of her. With renewed energy, he began thrusting.

"Prove it." She met his gaze, eyes wide open, and didn't look away.

"Will you come again?"

She arched into him. "Make me."

That was all it took. Deacon let go. His release hit him with the force of a speeding freight train. He thought Liberty might have climaxed again but was too caught up in his own pleasure to tell for sure.

Afterward, they cuddled for several long minutes, fingers linked, legs entwined. Because she suggested it, they took a shower, though washing up was forgotten when Deacon showed her just how incredible their wet bodies felt sliding against each other.

He toweled her off and watched contentedly when she borrowed his comb and toothbrush. Bedtime routines were infinitely more interesting when done naked.

She hadn't mentioned leaving or him taking her home. He was suddenly afraid she might. Next to making love to her, Deacon wanted nothing more than to wake up with her beside him.

When they finished in the bathroom, they fell into bed. Deacon tucked the sheets around her.

"Tired?"

He lay on his back, Liberty on her side. He draped an arm around her shoulders. She traced invisible circle eights on his chest and stomach.

"A little," she murmured sleepily. "Are you?"

"Getting there." He cranked his head sideways to look at the digital clock on the nightstand. "It's almost one. I can't believe it."

"Don't remind me." She groaned and covered her eyes.

"What time do you have to be up?"

She peeked at him through splayed fingers. "I'm not saying. It'll only depress me."

With the second day of the rodeo starting at nine, she'd have to be at work by the crack of dawn.

"Should you let your family know you're not coming home?"

"I'll text them in the morning. They're probably asleep by now."

"We should get some shut-eye, too." He kissed her forehead.

"Don't tell anyone about tonight, okay? In case Mercer hears. I don't want you getting in trouble with him."

"I won't mention it. But we were seen together at the Hole in the Wall."

"Dancing is one thing. Spending the night, another."

"I'm meeting with him on Monday. I would make it tomorrow, except he's going to be busy with the rodeo."

"Good," she murmured.

Deacon felt her head grow heavy on his arm.

He didn't remember falling asleep. The next thing he knew, Liberty bolted upright and a rooster was crowing somewhere nearby. A rooster? In his room?

"That's my cell phone," she said, and climbed out of bed. "Where are my clothes?"

Deacon reached for the lamp and switched it on.

Digging the phone out of her jeans pocket, she checked the display and rolled her eyes. "Damn, it's Cassidy."

The clock read 6:37 a.m. They'd overslept.

"Are you going to answer it?" Climbing out of bed, he found his own jeans and stepped into them. His shirt followed.

"Hello," Liberty said with exaggerated brightness. "I'm, uh, fine. Yeah, sorry. I fell asleep and forgot to set the alarm on my phone." She located her bra and panties and, balancing the phone in the crook of her neck, slipped into them. "No, I didn't. I'll tell you later. Really, I'm perfectly fine. Fabulous, in fact." She shot Deacon a smile. Then, her features promptly fell. "He what! No, I had no clue. Relax, Cassidy. Mom won't fire Tatum. She loves her like another daughter." Liberty's responses were clipped and terse. "I'll see you shortly. A half hour. Fine, fine. Twenty minutes."

"Everything okay?" he asked when she disconnected.

"I think so. Other than I have to explain my absence last night."

"I'm serious, honey."

"Honey?" She sidled over to him. "That's the first time you've called me that."

"Get used to it." He took her by the arms and kissed her briefly. He'd have liked to linger, but there wasn't time. "What's wrong?"

"Mercer and my mother apparently called my brother Ryder last night. They asked him to come home and help run the arena. With business increasing, Mercer thinks we could use a marketing expert."

"Is that what Ryder does?"

"According to Mercer, he's some kind of semi-genius." Liberty splashed water on her face, then ran the comb through her short blond hair. It lay in pretty waves, framing her face. Deacon liked the look, so different from her usual one.

"That's good, then." He used the comb after her, enjoying how easily they accomplished their morning routine together. Just like they had their bedtime one.

"It's great," she said. "I would *love* for Ryder to come home. That's one of the main reasons I've pushed my parents together. Except Cassidy's against it."

"Why?"

"She thinks Ryder will be a threat to Tatum's job."

"She runs the office."

"She also handles our marketing—what there is of it."

"But that's only a small part of her job, right?"

"Exactly!" Liberty shoved her feet into her boots.

They quickly finished dressing and headed out the door. Deacon held Liberty's hand the entire drive to the Easy Money.

A quarter mile away, the rooster crowed again. "Yeah, sis," she said into the phone, her voice strained. "We're almost there. Uh-huh. What?" As she listened, lines of consternation appeared on her brow. "He didn't! Oh, my God. I will. Yes, see you in a minute."

"Something else happen?" Deacon asked.

"Mercer came in while Mom and Cassidy were eating breakfast and announced that he's buying six bulls. Can you believe it? Mom came unglued, of course, and refused to authorize the expenditure. Then he told her he was using his own money. That's apparently why he wants Ryder home. He says bucking bulls will double or triple our revenue, which is why we need a full-time marketing expert."

"Ah."

"Ah? That's your response?"

"Are you surprised?" Deacon turned his truck into the arena driveway. "Mercer is a livestock foreman."

"But he can't buy bulls per the partnership agreement. I know. I read it."

"My guess is he's hoping to convince your mother to go along with him."

"Truthfully, I'm in favor of owning our own bulls. Especially if it brings Ryder home." She slumped in her seat. "But Mom is going to fight Mercer tooth and nail."

"He may have more influence on her than you think."

"What are *you* going to do?" she asked as Deacon parked next to her SUV.

"My job is to advise your dad to the best of my ability."

"I meant about us."

Deacon cut the engine, glad she considered them an "us" and glad she was concerned about their future. "I'm giving Mercer a month's notice. That's only fair. And I'll agree to work with whatever attorney he hires to replace me."

"Okay." She smiled happily.

"The bulls and your family, that's something you'll have to handle on your own. Even after Mercer and I officially part ways, I'll support you and be there for you, but it's best if I remain on the sidelines."

"You're right." She stared at the house, her breath escaping in a long sigh. "I'm not looking forward to this. Or the questions Mom and Cassidy will ask about us."

"How will you answer them?"

"Vaguely." She leaned across the console to place a light peck on his cheek. "I intend to leave them guessing as long as possible."

She was coming home at seven in the morning after being out all night. Deacon didn't think there'd be much guessing involved.

MORE OFTEN THAN NOT, the kitchen was the place where the Beckett women conducted their powwows. This morning was no exception.

Liberty sat at the table and sipped a cup of coffee, a morning ritual she'd forgone at Deacon's. The caffeine-infused brew was something she desperately needed. By her estimation, they'd managed barely five hours of sleep. What promised to be a long day was going to feel even longer as the hours dragged by.

"I don't like the way he...he...bribes us by suggesting Ryder come home, then drops the bombshell about the bulls." Cassidy scrubbed her face tiredly. She hadn't had much sleep, either. None of them had, apparently.

She'd propped Benjy in front of the TV with a bowl of cereal. It wasn't something she typically did. Cassidy hated using the TV as a babysitter, but today she'd made an exception. Because he was only a few feet away in the other room, they kept their voices at a reasonable level.

"And what about Tatum?" Cassidy continued. She sat across from their mother with Liberty in between.

"She'll always have a job here as long as she wants one," Sunny insisted. "Which I hope won't be long. The school board votes on the annual budget in a few months, and with luck, she'll have her old teaching position back. If not, she remains an Easy Money employee. Rest assured."

"What if Mercer says we can't afford her?" Cassidy asked. "Ryder won't be working for free, and I'm sure he'll be earning *considerably* more than Tatum."

"I run the office and admin side of the business. She will not be terminated. For any reason."

Cassidy appeared somewhat mollified.

"I want Ryder to come home," Liberty said, her voice thick with emotion. She blamed the lack of sleep. "My big brother…and I hardly know him. If buying a few bulls makes that happen, I vote yes."

"I want him home, too." Her mother also had a catch in her voice. "I haven't seen him in years. But I can't allow your father to manipulate me."

Liberty could relate. Mercer had manipulated her, too, using her to force his way back into their lives. There was no denying he was doing it again with her mother and the bulls.

But while his methods were questionable and not easy to forgive, his motives weren't. Like her, he wanted only to reunite the Becketts and, she was coming to realize, secure the future for his children and grandson. That wasn't such a horrible ambition.

"There has to be some compromise you two can reach," Liberty said.

Cassidy immediately countered her. "We swore we would never own any bulls again."

Liberty was tired of her sister constantly fighting their father at every step. "So, we have bulls again. Mercer's right. It will increase our revenue. We can have the best arena and best bucking horses in the state, but cowboys want bulls to ride, too."

"We have bulls. We lease them."

"Only during events. And we pay through the nose. With our own bulls, we can put on jackpots and charge for practice sessions."

"I appreciate what you're saying, sweetie." Sunny reached over and patted Liberty's hand. "For most livestock contractors, this would be a no-brainer. But if your father and I are to have a fair and equitable partnership, he must respect me. Not make decisions, especially bad ones, without my input or approval. That's what drove the business into the ground after he started drinking."

"He's in charge of the livestock operations," Liberty argued. "How is it he can't make decisions without your input or approval but you can without his? You just said Tatum would always have a job with us, no matter what."

"First of all, there's a big difference between Tatum and the bulls. She's family. Having bulls nearly ruined us."

"Was it really that bad?"

"You were young. You don't remember."

"I remember you were worried it *might* ruin us and relieved when it didn't."

"There were a few lean months. None of us wants to go through that again."

"Accidents like Ernie's are rare."

If it even was an accident. Liberty was having serious doubts.

"Bulls are expensive and high maintenance," Sunny said.

"Our costs will soar, and the increase in revenue may not be enough to cover them."

"It was before."

"The economy was different then."

"Without the bulls, there's no reason for Ryder to come home." Liberty's plea came straight from her heart. "I know you were angry at first, maybe still are, that I contacted Mercer without your knowledge. But this is a chance for the whole family to be together again. I thought you wanted that."

"Of course I want that."

"Then say yes."

"I can't allow your father to buy the bulls with his own money. Per the partnership agreement, that will give him a greater share of the business assets. I don't have the funds myself to match that purchase."

"Okay, so he owns a tiny larger portion of the business."

Her mother abruptly straightened. "That will not happen. I have to set the precedent now or he'll steamroller me on every decision."

"Hear, hear," Cassidy seconded.

She and their mother promptly engaged in a one-sided debate that excluded Liberty.

"Owning bulls presents a whole new set of problems." Sunny ticked the items off on her fingers. "Our insurance policy would have to be requoted. Workmen's compensation, too. Bull riding is the most dangerous of all rodeo events. Our liability waivers would need updating. The bulls we lease are fully covered by the various stock contractors. Not to mention the feed bill. Bulls eat an enormous amount."

"Remember," Cassidy said, "we used to have a full-time bull handler. We'd need one again. That's another expense."

Liberty blew out a long, frustrated breath. They were making excuses. Given time, they'd manufacture a dozen more.

"Mercer can handle the bulls," she said.

"What about when Walter retires?" Her mother pushed away from the table.

Yet another excuse. "Why are you suddenly opposing Mercer?"

"This is hardly sudden."

"Seems to me you two have been getting along pretty good lately. I saw you kissing him yesterday," Liberty said.

Cassidy gasped. "You kissed him?"

"It's not what you think."

"Seriously, Mom. There's only one way to interpret a kiss." Was it Liberty's imagination, or was her mother blushing? "You still love him. Admit it."

"A part of me will always love him. But we're not *in* love and not a couple."

"Not yet."

"Definitely not if he purchases those bulls without my consent." She dumped her empty coffee mug in the sink. It banged against the other dishes.

For a moment, they were all silent. A knock sounded at the kitchen door, causing Liberty to jump. Was it Mercer?

Kenny's smiling face greeted her mother when she opened the door. "Hate to bother you, Sunny, but the battery's dead in the tractor, and I need to grade the arena."

"Where's Mercer?"

"Can't find him. Or a pair of jumper cables."

"I have some in my car. Be right back," she said over her shoulder. "You two, shake a leg. The food and merchandise vendors have already arrived, and the entrance gate opens in twenty minutes."

Liberty checked the microwave clock and silently groaned. Disposing of her own mug—more gently—she started for her bedroom and the change of clothes she desperately needed. She didn't get far.

"What's with you and Deacon?" Cassidy stopped her in the hall. "I heard you two were dancing up a storm at the Hole in the Wall last night. Then you didn't come home."

"I fell asleep."

"On his couch or in his bed?"

"When he brought me home last night, Mercer's truck was in the driveway." Liberty leaned against the wall. "I didn't want to walk in on him and Mom, so Deacon took me back to his place. We talked."

"Talked. Right."

"It's not what you think," Liberty said, echoing her mother. Did she sound as lame?

"I like Deacon, I told you that before. But he's Dad's attorney."

"Not for long."

"You're crossing a line," her sister warned.

"Soon, there'll be no line. Deacon promised."

"Men disappoint you."

Was that a reference to the man who had fathered her child and broken her heart?

"If I were you, I'd worry more about Mom and Mercer and less about me and Deacon."

There was genuine compassion and concern in Cassidy's voice when she spoke. "I hope you're right, little sister. I truly do."

Liberty hoped so, too, and that she didn't come to regret the day she'd tracked Mercer down and invited him to Reckless.

Chapter Thirteen

On Monday at 9:27 a.m. sharp Mercer presented himself at Deacon's office. Anna Maria showed him in, her darkly penciled brows drawn together in a severe V.

What, Deacon wondered, had Mercer said to his secretary to worry her?

"We need to talk," Mercer announced without preamble.

They did, which was why Deacon had scheduled the appointment to terminate their contract yesterday at the rodeo. Not wishing to alert his client, he'd cited a routine reason.

Given Mercer's apparent anger, he'd either discovered Deacon's true purpose or something else had happened.

"About what?" he asked.

Mercer waved a hand in the air. "I need you to do whatever it is you attorneys do to sever the partnership agreement between me and Sunny."

Deacon had been standing when Mercer entered his office. At his client's demand he sat—*plunked* was a better description—into his chair. He'd anticipated the meeting not going well. Now he was certain of it but for different reasons.

"It's called a dissolution." He took a moment to organize his thoughts. "And it's nothing you want to rush into."

"I'm not rushing. I've thought about nothing else since yesterday."

"Is this abrupt change because Sunny objects to you buying the bulls"

"Damn straight."

Liberty and Deacon had spoken briefly yesterday at the rodeo and again a couple of hours ago, right before her first riding class. She'd told him about her mother and Mercer arguing off and on all day yesterday and again this morning. Also about the heated discussion she'd had with her mother and sister.

Deacon had glimpsed the steel that lay beneath Mercer's affable manner the other day when he warned Deacon to stay away from Liberty. Apparently, two days of arguing with his ex only hardened that metal.

"I advise against it, Mercer. You and Sunny running the arena together is in both of your best interests."

"Sunny is wrong."

"And Liberty's right. You coerce people into doing what you want. It's one thing in business, another thing entirely when it comes to family."

"This *is* business."

"It's more than that."

"Sunny's been in charge of the arena a long time. She has to understand she has a partner now."

"The way to make her understand isn't to dissolve your partnership."

"She'll concede before it comes to that."

"You're taking a huge risk." Deacon decided to stop tiptoeing around the older man. "You'll not only drive a permanent wedge between you and Sunny, you'll drive one between you and your daughters."

"Liberty sides with me. She said so herself."

"Yes, when it comes to expanding the bucking stock operation. Not with your tactics. If you hurt Sunny and make her unhappy, I guarantee Liberty will stop siding with you in a heartbeat. She loves her mother, despite their recent difficulties."

"You call lying to her all her life a difficulty?"

"She won't choose you over Sunny in the end. She doesn't have the same feelings for you."

Mercer's features fell. A moment later, the snarl was back in his bark. "I'm sick and tired of Sunny holding my drinking against me. I've proved over and over I'm reformed."

"You have. But threatening her isn't the solution."

"If she wants to be in charge of the arena that badly, she can. I'll just leave and take the money she owes me."

Whatever was going on with Sunny and Mercer went beyond the bulls. They were simply using them as a battleground for their personal war. Unfortunately, their children and grandson were the ones suffering—not to mention their business.

"I saw you kissing Sunny."

"You did?" Some of Mercer's bluster deserted him.

"Liberty saw, too."

He made a disgruntled sound under his breath.

"You and Sunny have a lot of history together. Falling into old habits is natural."

"Kissing her wasn't an old habit."

"For you. Maybe for her it was. She could have been testing the waters or satisfying her curiosity."

"What are you, a therapist as well as an attorney?"

Sometimes. It came with the job; however, admitting as much wouldn't win Deacon points, and he preferred not to antagonize Mercer. He was already perturbed, and there was still the termination of their representation contract to discuss.

"I strongly suggest you take a few days to consider this. Surely that won't make any difference. Talk to Sunny and your daughters. Not argue."

"Can't." Mercer shook his head. "The livestock broker gave me until five o'clock today or he'll sell the bulls to the next buyer in line. A bargain like this doesn't come around very often."

"Can you buy the bulls and keep them somewhere else? Just until Sunny relents?"

"What good is that?" Mercer snorted. "The whole purpose of buying them is to increase revenues. I want you to prepare the dissolution and deliver it to Sunny by this afternoon."

What would Liberty say to that? Nothing good. She'd feel betrayed, naturally. Not two nights ago he'd assured her he was terminating his relationship with her father and clearing the path for them. Worse, Deacon would be an instrument in helping Mercer tear the Becketts further apart.

"No," he said. "I won't do it."

"You have to. You're my attorney. You work for me."

"Not anymore. Consider this my notice."

Deacon had planned on giving Mercer thirty days. In light of this recent development, he didn't deserve it.

"Did Liberty put you up to this?" Surprise, then anger, flared in Mercer's eyes. "I heard you two have been keeping company despite what I told you."

Deacon braced himself. "My personal life is off-limits."

"You wouldn't be doing this if not for her."

"Under *any* circumstances I would be advising you against dissolving your partnership agreement with Sunny. It's a bad idea. You're acting out of anger because she rejected you."

He leaned forward and pounded Deacon's desk. "She did not reject me. It wasn't like that."

Not true. Mercer was overconfident. It went along with his need to control others. He'd figured one kiss and Sunny would automatically toe the line. Only she hadn't.

"I want that dissolution delivered today," he demanded in a raised voice.

Deacon didn't budge. "There's an attorney in Globe I recommend. She can prepare the necessary document and deliver it."

"That'll waste time."

"You're making a mistake, and I won't be a part of it."

"You will." Mercer stood. "Or I'll call the bar association and report you. I'm pretty sure that sleeping with your client's daughter is against some kind of code or rule."

"You don't know what went on between us."

"I can make a pretty good guess."

Deacon felt as if he'd hit the ground hard after being thrown from a second-story window. If Mercer made that call, there would be an inquiry. Possibly an investigation. His license to practice law could be suspended.

"Mercer, I—"

"Call me when you've delivered the dissolution to Sunny." He didn't wait for Deacon to reply and stormed out of the office.

"Everything okay?" Anna Maria asked a few minutes later.

How much, if anything, had she heard?

"Yeah. Can you call and reschedule my ten-o'clock for tomorrow? My one-o'clock, too. And hold my calls."

"Sure. Let me know if you need anything else."

He would. He'd need her to type up the letter notifying Sunny that Mercer was formally dissolving their partnership.

As much as Deacon disagreed with his client, and as much as he didn't want to do this for Liberty and her family's sake, he had no choice. He'd worked too hard and too long, endured too many hardships, to jeopardize his career.

Liberty would have to understand that Mercer had

strong-armed him with threats just like her and the rest of the Beckett women.

There was, however, one important difference. Deacon had only himself to blame for the position he was in. He'd spent the night with Liberty knowing full well it was wrong, and now he was going to pay the price. They both were.

"CAN HE DO THIS?" Sunny sat at her desk, reading the partnership dissolution letter.

"I recommend you seek the council of your own attorney," Deacon said.

"Quit the legal mumbo jumbo and tell me." She glared at him, angrily but not accusingly.

"He can, and I'm afraid he will." Deacon had come to their meeting wearing his game face. He hoped it was still in place. "The way the agreement is worded, either partner can dissolve the partnership simply by giving notice."

"What do I do?" The letter floated to the desktop, and her head fell into her waiting hands. "He'll demand the money I owe him. Bankrupt us. Just like before."

Here we go again, Deacon thought. He could fault Mercer plenty for his unashamed audacity, but he'd take that any day over Sunny and her melodramatics.

Poor Liberty, being saddled with these two.

"No disrespect intended, but you should have thought of that before you refused."

Her head shot up. "Excuse me!"

In the distance, thunder boomed. The monsoon season, almost at an end, was sending them a final downpour. How appropriate.

"Is it the bulls you're afraid of, or something else?"

"I don't like what you're implying." Her voice went from desperate to sharp.

"Then I'll take my leave." He picked up his briefcase

and started for the door, more than ready to be done with the Becketts.

Truth be told, he was fed up with both Mercer's and Sunny's antics. They were selfish, spiteful and cared only for themselves while pretending to care for others.

His parents were equally selfish. They, at least, didn't hide behind pretenses.

At that moment, the office door flew open, and Liberty tumbled inside. "Where is it?" she demanded. "Let me see."

Sunny had telephoned her daughters the minute Deacon presented her with the dissolution letter. Cassidy and Benjy were shopping for school supplies with Tatum and her brood. Liberty was apparently nearer.

Deacon had searched for her when he first arrived at the arena. While he couldn't have revealed the contents of the letter, he'd wanted to prepare her for bad news. Luck wasn't on his side—she'd been nowhere around.

Sunny passed the letter to Liberty. Her complexion paled as she read it. "What in God's name is he doing?"

Tearing his family apart, in Deacon's opinion. "You'll have to ask him."

Though it troubled Deacon to leave her in such an obvious state of distress, he squeezed past her toward the door. "I'm sorry."

The apology was hardly adequate to make up for her misery. It was, however, the most he could offer at the moment.

He'd barely reached his truck when she came up behind him.

"How could you?" she demanded.

What? Disappoint her? Fail her? Break his promise? He picked delivering the letter to dissolve their partnership.

"I had no choice." Facing her was difficult. Deacon did it anyway. She deserved more from him than to speak to his back.

"You could have refused."

Telling her that Mercer threatened to report him to the bar association would be shifting the blame from himself and taking the coward's way out. Deacon would have none of it.

"I work for your father. As long as what he asks of me isn't illegal or fraudulent, it's my duty, my obligation, to comply."

"You said you were going to terminate your relationship with him."

"I gave him my notice. He didn't accept it."

"Does he have a choice?"

"Delivering the letter to your mother was my last official task for him. I advised against it, tried to change his mind. He was adamant."

"I still don't understand." She pressed the heel of her hand into her forehead.

"Your father is no dummy, and he persuaded me rather convincingly."

"He did more than persuade. I'm one of his victims, remember?" Her hand dropped limply to her side. "What hammer did he hold over your head? Me?"

"I can't discuss that with you."

"Seriously, Deacon? You're going to pull that attorney-client privilege BS on me now of all times?"

"It's not BS."

"Mom doesn't have the money. Dissolving the partnership could ruin our business."

"It could."

"And, yet, you delivered the letter."

"This is a delicate situation, one that could go very wrong, very fast." He gentled his voice. "Trust me, when this is over in a week or a month—"

"I thought I was important to you."

"You are. But our relationship isn't the only thing at stake."

"What else is?"

"I'm trying to protect you."

She backed away. "And yourself."

"That isn't fair."

"You're right." She blinked the tears from her eyes. "I've been battered and beaten up by both my parents. My mother lied to me, and the father I only just met used me. On top of that, my sister's angry. Constantly. And my brother goes out of his way to avoid us. Still, all I want is for us to be one big happy family. Stupid, right? Then you come along, and I think you're the kind of guy I've been waiting to meet. Except you work for my father. Who apparently doesn't give a damn about me or he wouldn't have forced you to choose between us."

"First of all, I didn't choose him over you."

"Feels like you did."

"In his way, he's trying to do what's best for everyone. Namely, grow the family business."

"You're defending him!"

"His motives, not his methods. Your mother's no different. She also wants what's best. Only her ideas are the polar opposite of Mercer's. That leaves the rest of us caught in the middle."

In the cross fire was more like it.

"Let's leave. Today." She clutched at his shirtsleeve with frantic fingers. "Phoenix. Tucson. California. It doesn't matter."

"Running away won't solve anything."

"It worked for you."

"By some miracle."

She released his sleeve with a jerking motion that might as well have been a slap to his face.

"There's nothing I'd love more than to go away with

you," he said. "Honestly. But we're not teenagers, and the problems with your parents won't disappear just because we do. There's also my reputation."

"What difference will it make if we leave?"

"It'll make a difference to me."

"You think I'm being immature."

"Hardly." No more game face. He wanted Liberty to see for herself his true feelings. "You're the first woman I've met whom I've wanted to have a lasting relationship with. That wasn't possible before you, and not because someone broke my heart. My parents did that. I haven't forgotten the damage they inflicted, but I've moved past it. If not, I wouldn't be standing here, desperate to hold you and going crazy because I can't."

"You don't think I'm capable of having a real, lasting relationship with you until my family is fixed?"

"Do you?"

"What if they're not fixable?" She wiped at her damp cheeks.

"Maybe you're trying too hard. Instead of reconciling your parents, help them learn how to work together. As partners, not adversaries."

Lightning flashed on the horizon, followed by a loud clap of thunder. In another minute, the rain would fall. Riders scrambled to put their horses up before getting soaked.

Deacon and Liberty didn't move.

"What about us?" she asked.

"We need to wait until this latest upheaval with your parents plays out." And until he was confident there would be no repercussions from Mercer. "We can't afford to make another mistake."

She bristled. "Is that what the other night was? A mistake?"

"No." He winced. "Poor choice of words."

"Or just a poor choice."

"You know that's not true."

"To be honest, I'm not sure."

Deacon didn't let her remark affect him. Her world had been turned upside down for a second time in a month. She was allowed to fire a few arrows.

It was tempting to reveal Mercer's threat. Then she'd hate him and not Deacon. Except he believed what he'd told her before. They couldn't move ahead until, as she put it, her family was fixed.

"Be patient," he said.

"Argh! I'm tired of being patient, and tired of them controlling my life."

"They get away with it because we let them."

"And breaking up with me will stop it?"

"Not a breakup."

"Breathing room. Space. A time-out?"

"Something like that."

"Giving it some cutesy name doesn't make it any better. Or hurt any less."

"Your parents are using our relationship against us."

"They wouldn't if we stood up to them."

"*You* need to do it more than me."

She reeled as if shoved in the chest. "This isn't my fault!"

"Of course not. That's not what I meant. I'm just as responsible as you. More."

"Another poor choice of words?"

"I'm sorry." He was saying that a lot.

"An apology makes everything better," she said tightly, and turned to go.

"Please. Wait."

"Forget it." She shook her head. "I was a fool to have gone home with you."

If she was trying to wound him, it was working. "Liberty, wait." He raised his hand toward her. "Honey."

Her features crumpled, and she fled, disappearing into the office.

Deacon debated going after her, but even if she'd listen, she wouldn't take him back. Not after his world-class blunder. How could he have even remotely insinuated she was to blame for what happened?

Getting into his truck, he drove away. On the day he'd signed the representation contract with Mercer, he'd resigned himself to the fact Liberty Beckett was off-limits. He should have stuck to his guns. Then neither of them would be running for emotional cover, and he wouldn't be doing a damn fine job of living up to his old nickname.

Chapter Fourteen

"Is there anything else you need?" Anna Maria laid the completed motion to proceed on Deacon's desk.

"That's all for now. Thanks." He smiled. It was shallow at best.

"I'll finish updating your calendar before I leave." She closed the office door behind her.

Deacon studied the court document in front of him, for all the good it did. The letters refused to remain in focus. The malady had been plaguing him since his breakup with Liberty.

Breakup. Not breathing room or space or a time-out. He'd abandoned that notion when she continually refused to take his phone calls. Three days ago, he quit trying.

He caught periodic glimpses of her when he was at the arena exercising Huck and Confetti. He didn't have to work hard at avoiding her, since she was doing a stellar job of keeping her distance. One evening he joined the team penning practice, secretly hoping she'd make an appearance. Halfway through, he'd spotted her SUV driving off.

He worried that she was okay and, biting the bullet, asked Mercer about her. The other man had nothing to offer. It seemed Liberty refused to speak to him, too, except for arena business, and then only when absolutely necessary.

Mercer's pressure tactics had prevailed, and Sunny

folded. The bulls, six in total, had arrived the day before yesterday amid tremendous fanfare. Sunny might not be happy about the arena's newest additions, but everyone else was. Mercer had informed Deacon yesterday that they'd landed several new lucrative bucking stock contracts and entries were maxed out for their first bull riding jackpot next week.

Like Liberty, Deacon spoke to Mercer only when necessary. Though he'd promised to work with whatever attorney Mercer hired to replace him, that had yet to happen. Mercer was stonewalling. Typical of him.

Deacon wasn't sure he'd attend the bull riding jackpot. He'd been considering closing his practice and leaving Reckless. His friend Murry had made him a generous offer to join his firm as a junior partner. Deacon kept telling himself that changing jobs was a smart career move. New town. Fresh faces. Interesting challenges.

There was still the matter of clearing his name, which he hadn't done and wouldn't if he moved. Weeks of asking questions had only resulted in more questions than answers. At this point, it was unlikely he'd ever find out what really happened.

And unlikely he'd expand his practice. Another reason to accept Murry's offer and relocate.

Dammit. He should have waited before taking Liberty to his bed and taking her into his heart. Then, he wouldn't have made impossible promises, only to disappoint her. No wonder she didn't trust him, and no wonder he'd lost her.

Leaving Reckless probably was for the best.

You're running away again.

He'd told Liberty that wasn't the solution when she'd suggested it. But these were different circumstances. A good job waited for him, one with enormous potential.

You're taking the easy way out.

This particular self-criticism was a little harder to explain away. He'd been angry at Sunny for not standing by him after the accident when he should be angry at himself for not staying and fighting. Leaving had made it easy for people to blame him.

What might have happened if he'd stayed? Hard to say. He wasn't the same person as before. His priorities had changed and his past no longer defined him.

Eduardo Frias had taught him that last lesson. Would he be disappointed in Deacon for leaving Reckless? That merited some rumination. Over a beer maybe. Deacon could be done for the day, if he chose, and the Hole in the Wall was just up the street. A short walk.

He hadn't been there since the night with Liberty. Memories assailed him the instant he walked through the door. Being a weeknight and with no rodeo in town, the place was filled with mostly regulars.

Deacon claimed an empty bar stool for himself and ordered a draft beer.

"You meeting someone?"

He turned to see Ernie Tuckerman standing there. Where had he come from? "No."

"Do you mind?"

Ernie was already sliding onto the neighboring bar stool before Deacon could say, "Have a seat."

He struggled to find a comfortable position. His bum leg stuck out in front of him at an awkward angle.

Why had he joined Deacon? Their last encounter, not fifteen feet from here, was anything but social.

Ernie didn't make him wait long for the answer. "Your friend Murry came by to see me today. The Social Security Administration has offered a settlement."

The sum he named had Deacon whistling softly. Ernie could accomplish a lot with that money. Improve his living conditions for starters. "Congratulations. I'm glad to hear it."

"Are you? Glad?"

"You were unfairly denied benefits for several years. The money was owed you."

"You didn't have to help me. Most guys in your shoes would have told me where to shove it."

"We're not teenagers anymore."

"What Liberty said the other day, she was right. I was ungrateful. And rude."

"You were angry. And you blamed me for what happened."

He reached into his shirt pocket and removed an envelope. From that, he withdrew three sheets of paper and laid them flat on the bar. Deacon recognized the acceptance letter from Social Security.

"I haven't signed this yet. I can't."

"Why not?"

Ernie smoothed the already flat pages, his gaze fixed on them. "There's something I have to get off my chest first. Something important."

"Okay."

"I know you didn't cause the accident."

Had all Deacon's poking and prodding finally netted results?

"How's that?"

Ernie's hand trembled slightly as he fingered the pages. Nerves? A residual effect of his injuries? "I accused you before anyone could accuse me."

Deacon didn't move. Didn't dare speak. It was important for him to hear every word of Ernie's confession. Vitally important.

"I'm the one who opened the gates," Ernie said. "Tank used the electric shocker on Heavy Metal and a couple of the other bulls. Got them good and mad so they'd charge."

"Why?"

Ernie laughed bitterly. "I didn't think anyone would get

hurt. Least of all me. I told Tank to wait until I was out of the way. Guess he didn't hear me or got in a hurry."

"That's crazy."

"Yeah, tell me about it. I figured the bulls would run amok for a few minutes. We'd have us a time rounding them up, and you'd land in trouble. Maybe lose your job."

"You almost died."

"That'll teach me to play a prank."

"A prank?" Deacon set his mug down, having lost all taste for his beer. "Did you hate me that much?"

Ernie glanced away, then back at Deacon. "Not hate. But I was damn sure jealous of you."

"For what?"

"You were a better bull rider than me. I overheard Joe Blackwood telling Sunny how you had the best chance of coming home with a state championship." Pain ravaged his features. "I was stupid. It should have been me they were calling Einstein. Not you."

Liberty had implicated Ernie in the accident, but Deacon had talked himself out of the possibility. One more mistake he'd made.

"When I woke up in the hospital after the surgery, I panicked," Ernie continued. "I didn't want anyone thinking I caused the accident so I blamed you. What I should have been doing was worrying about how I'd ruined my life. Can't even ride a horse these days, much less rodeo."

If Deacon had considered Ernie's accident a tragedy before, he considered it doubly so now.

"I want to pay you for the work you did on my case." Ernie nudged the pages toward Deacon. "I'm thinking we could split this fifty-fifty."

"I don't want your money."

"You deserve it for what I've put you through."

Deacon took a moment to consider his response. He

was tired of carrying a grudge. It had darkened his life for far too long.

"Things weren't easy for me after I left Reckless. In fact, they were pretty shitty. But I might not have the career I do now if I'd stayed."

"I'll make sure everyone in town knows the truth."

"You don't have to."

"I do. Especially the Becketts. I'll drop by the arena tomorrow afternoon."

Deacon understood then. Ernie had a moral compass. He just hadn't been following it for a while. Coming clean was his way of putting himself back on course.

"I'll tell you what you can do with some of that money." Deacon raised his mug. "Buy the next round."

Ernie nodded. When he spoke, it was with difficulty. "It'd be my pleasure."

Deacon tapped the logo on the envelope. "They're a good legal firm."

"Sure did right by me."

"They offered me a job."

"You accept?"

"Not yet."

"Well, good luck to you. Folks in Reckless are going to miss you."

He'd miss them, too.

After the next round, Deacon left the honky-tonk. He and Ernie didn't part friends. Neither did they part enemies. A step in the right direction.

Deacon decided to return to his office and finish reviewing that motion to proceed Anna Maria had prepared before heading home. He'd hardly started when the phone rang. It was Murry.

"Hey, buddy."

"You're working late."

"I could say the same for you."

Deacon checked his watch. Any other evening, he might have run over to the Easy Money for a quick ride.

What would he do with his horses if he left Reckless and took that job with Murry's firm? There were plenty of places in the Phoenix metropolitan area to board them and ride. Some as nice as the Easy Money, if lacking their colorful, Wild West history.

"I saw Ernie Tuckerman a while ago," Deacon said. "He told me about the settlement offer. Nicely done."

"Speaking of which, have you given any more thought to the job?"

Deacon leaned back in his chair and propped his legs on his desk. "As a matter of fact, I've made a decision."

LIBERTY WATCHED ERNIE Tuckerman limp back to his junk-yard reject car, still in a state of profound awe. She'd always believed in Deacon's innocence and that Ernie was somehow involved in the accident. Not once did she imagine Ernie admitting his role and apologizing.

Even more astounding, Deacon was closing his practice and leaving Reckless. Ernie mentioned that last part almost as an afterthought. Liberty had tried to hide her reaction. It wasn't easy with four pairs of eyes studying her like a slide under a microscope. Family could be very intrusive at times.

"That took courage," Mercer said to no one in particular. "He didn't have to come forward. And he sure didn't have to tell us face-to-face."

"I'm glad we can finally put this to bed once and for all." Sunny rose from the picnic table and, bracing her hands on her hips, gazed in the direction of the bull pen on the other side of the arena.

The six enormous beasts were lying down and quietly chewing their cud, probably relieved the excitement surrounding their arrival three days ago had finally died down.

"Maybe now you'll be less worried about them." Mercer went over to stand beside her.

They'd gathered at the picnic table and chairs outside the office for the impromptu meeting with Ernie. There was no forethought involved. The spot simply happened to be where he'd caught up with Liberty's parents and where she and Cassidy joined them.

Sunny turned and gave Mercer "the look." "I agreed not to fight you on the bulls and you agreed not to dissolve our partnership. Doesn't mean I feel any better about having them on the property."

"You will when you see the money rolling in."

Liberty exchanged glances with her sister. Their parents' constant bickering strained their collective patience to its limit. Matchmaking? What had she been thinking? There was no reconciling that pair. Not while they continued with their ridiculous power struggle.

Deacon's sage advice rang in her ears. She *was* better off helping her parents work together rather than rekindling a romance that died twenty-five years ago.

God, she missed him. Ten whole days since their awful, terrible fight.

Nothing had turned out the way she'd envisioned it. She didn't have a loving or even affectionate relationship with her father—too many open, bleeding wounds. She'd yet to forgive her mother for lying to her all these years—same reason as above. And her family wasn't reconciled.

Well, not entirely accurate. Ryder was coming home. He'd called this morning to report he'd given his notice at his job and would arrive within the month.

Mercer's doing. Yay, one good thing to his credit.

Okay, okay, Ryder's return was wonderful. As was that small period of time when she and Deacon had been a couple.

Why hadn't she returned his phone calls? Ignoring him

had been unkind, and she wasn't an unkind person. But she'd been hurt and confused and the dissolution letter he'd delivered had been like a hurricane tearing through her family's lives.

Mercer's doing again. He'd put Deacon in a difficult position.

So had she. Deacon made her a promise, but she'd as much as forced it out of him. After she'd practically seduced him when she knew it would compromise his ethics. Deacon was an honorable attorney, and she hadn't respected that. It took Liberty a full week to put on her big-girl panties and admit her share of the blame.

Now, he was leaving town, and she'd never get the chance to tell him.

Liberty pressed a hand to her middle and the large knot of pain that had taken up permanent residence there.

Damn her parents. Damn her for being such a weakling. Instead of confronting them about their deceptions, she just kept hoping they'd reconcile. That way, things wouldn't have to get ugly or messy.

How wrong could she have been? The truth was, things needed to get really ugly and messy. Like cauterizing a wound.

She could do it. Stand up to her parents. Hold them accountable. Just not here and not now. Tomorrow, after she'd collected her thoughts and rehearsed a few mental speeches.

More hiding her head in the sand?

No, she told herself. Flying off the handle would serve no purpose. A ride in the hills—that was what she needed to calm her nerves and clear her head. It was still hot outside. She'd have to bring plenty of water.

"You mind covering my class for me?" she asked Cassidy.

"Sure. What's up?"

"Be back around seven." Liberty walked away, picturing their confused and annoyed expressions. Her mother's might be sympathetic. Sunny had felt bad that Deacon was leaving. Liberty had watched her closely after Ernie's announcement.

The latch to her mare's stall stuck and refused to budge. Liberty shoved hard, putting her weight in it. Finally, the latch gave. The effort drained her. Covering her face with her hands, she succumbed to the sobs she'd been holding back for over a week. The startled mare snorted and retreated to a far corner.

"You all right, darling?"

Her mother! Cripes. The woman had a knack for picking the worst possible times.

"Fine." Peachy. Never better.

"Are you sure?"

Liberty averted her head. "I'm going for a ride."

"Can we talk first?"

"Not now, Mom. Please. I'm kind of busy."

"I'm sorry I lied to you about Mercer being your father." Her mother sounded on the verge of tears herself. "I've done you both a disservice."

She'd heard the apology before. It should be enough to assuage her anger. It wasn't.

"Yes, you have." She expected her mother to ask for forgiveness, and was totally shocked when she didn't.

"You've done a disservice, as well."

"Hey, I'm the victim here!"

"You expect too much from us. From Deacon, too."

He'd said something similar. It stung as much then as now. "I think being told the truth about my father isn't expecting too much."

"I was protecting you. *Selfishly* protecting you," her mother amended before Liberty could object. "You have no idea what it was like. I loved Mercer more than life itself. I was certain if I let him stay, let him come back after he left, that he'd hurt us, me, all over again." Her voice cracked. "Only this time, the results might be worse than simply losing the arena."

"Are you referring to the night he crashed into the well house?"

"Can you imagine the outcome if he'd been driving on the road? Or going faster?" Her mother shuddered. "I could have lost a daughter. Or both of them."

"I'd have sent him away, too, after that. But I also would have told my other daughter that he was her biological father. Not some stranger."

"I was afraid you'd do exactly what you did and insist on meeting him. Maybe leave us to go live with him like Ryder had. I was *most* afraid he'd do what he did and come back to Reckless."

"You didn't pay him the money he was owed. You had to know he'd return eventually."

"As they say, out of sight, out of mind."

Obviously, Liberty inherited her head-in-the-sand tendency from her mother.

"That's not like you, Mom. You're smart."

She smiled ruefully. "Mercer does that to me. Makes me lose my head."

Liberty clearly inherited that tendency from her mother, too. She'd lost her head over Deacon. She'd thought only of the moment and not the consequences of their actions.

"I can't undo the past," Sunny said. "Can't give you back all those years with Mercer you lost. But I can give you the future."

Liberty shut the latch on the stall door. She wasn't going riding tonight. "I'm listening."

"He and I won't be reconciling. I know that's what you want."

"I never said—"

"Cassidy told me. She was quite appalled."

Though the remark was made in jest, Liberty couldn't bring herself to laugh. "It was a stupid idea."

"It was a sweet idea."

"I just wanted my parents back together. Is that so wrong?"

"Not at all." Her mother tucked a lock of hair behind Liberty's ear, the gesture familiar and endearing. "But Mercer and I, there's just too much bad history. I will promise you something, however."

Not another promise. She was through demanding those for a while.

"He and I are committed to making the Easy Money the best it can be. A successful, thriving business worthy of passing down to our children and grandchildren. To that end, we will strive to get along. If it kills us," she added through gritted teeth.

"Knowing how the two of you fight, that just might happen."

"Cassidy's also agreed to play nice with him. As best she can."

"That's good. I'd hate for Ryder to come home and find us at each other's throats."

"If he'd known about you, wild horses wouldn't have kept him away."

She was referring to Mercer, not Ryder. "He doesn't love me."

"He does. Trust me, I know the man. His intentions weren't to hurt you."

"That's what people keep saying." She was remembering Deacon. "But it hurt like hell anyway."

"We've let our bad history bleed over onto our children. It's shameful."

"It's a lot more than shameful, Mom." Liberty gave voice to her anger. It was satisfying and freeing. "Tossing out a few apologies doesn't make it any better."

"I know I have a lot of lost ground to recover."

"You've acted in your own best interests for years, telling yourself and the rest of us you were doing it to protect us. What mother denies her child her father? Even if he isn't such a great one. That's not shameful, Mom, it's despicable."

"You're right. I let my fears cloud my judgment. But they weren't completely unjustified. Mercer did nearly bankrupt the arena, and he did endanger your sister."

Liberty's shoulders slumped. Her outburst had taken some of the wind from her sails. "What's changed you all of a sudden?"

"That's a fair question."

"Oh, don't tell me. It was Ernie admitting he let the bulls out. Not Deacon."

"No. It was seeing how devastated you are over losing Deacon. A mother dreams of the day her daughter falls in love with a wonderful man. She doesn't dream of being the impetus that drives her daughter and that man apart. If I could turn back time to the day he delivered the dissolution letter, I would."

Fresh tears pricked Liberty's eyes. She did love Deacon. More than she'd thought it was possible. Finally, Liberty Beckett falls for a guy, then goes and sabotages it.

"I messed things up with him. Not you and Mercer."

"You had lots of help."

She sniffed. "We do seem dedicated to making each other miserable."

"I want you to be happy, sweetie. For all of us to be happy. And to make up for the heartache I've caused."

Liberty could hold out longer. She definitely had it in her. Was that really what she wanted? A family perpetually torn apart because she was too stubborn to forgive?

Her mother was trying. The least Liberty could do was try, too.

She opened her arms. The next instant, she and her mother were embracing, the first time since before Mercer's return. It felt good. And natural. There was yet hope for the Becketts.

After shedding a few more tears, the two of them chatted like mother and daughter, setting tentative plans for when Ryder arrived. Liberty wanted to share her mother's excitement. It was hard.

"I'll see you at dinner, okay?" Having canceled her ride, she decided to accomplish a few of Cassidy's chores. She owed her sister that much for covering her class.

"Mercer wants to talk to you," Sunny said.

Liberty wanted to talk to him, too. When she wasn't such an emotional wreck. "I will. Later."

"He's waiting for you."

She stared down the barn aisle. True to her mother's words, Mercer stood at the entrance to the barn. Ducking out without him seeing her was impossible.

Big deal. Did she care?

To her surprise, she realized she did.

Chapter Fifteen

"I didn't want to interrupt you and your mother," Mercer said when Liberty neared.

What was this? Parents-gang-up-on-their-daughter day?

She opened the door to the tack room, which was where they also kept their medical supplies. "I have to put some liniment on Diablo's legs and wrap them."

"I'll help."

"It's a one-person job, Mercer."

"Then I'll talk while you work."

She sighed. He was harder to shake than a hungry stray dog.

But hadn't she just made a commitment to reunite her family? That couldn't happen if she kept ignoring Mercer.

"Give me a minute." She gathered the bottle of liniment, four pads and four leg wraps."

"Let me carry that." He held out his hands.

"No need." Balancing the items awkwardly against her chest—she could be pigheaded right up there with the best of them—she forged ahead.

Mercer followed her not only to Diablo's stall but into the stall with her. There, he hovered as she inspected the horse's legs for lingering signs of stiffness.

Liberty straightened. "I'm waiting, Mercer."

He met her gaze directly. "I love your mother. Almost

everything I've done, good and bad, has been because I want to get her back."

"It's the bad stuff I have a problem with."

"I deserve your anger. We can sort through that later, however."

"Isn't that why we're here? To sort through my anger?" She grabbed the liniment and started applying it to Diablo's back legs.

"I want to talk about Deacon."

She tottered precariously for a fraction of a second before steadying herself. "Well, I don't."

"I get mad, and I convince myself I can get people to do what I want by pressuring them."

"You're only just realizing that?"

He chuckled.

"I wasn't joking."

"No, I don't guess you were." He leaned an elbow on the stall door. "I figured out how obnoxious I can be twenty-five years ago when your mother kicked me to the curb. Which I heartily deserved, by the way."

"What does this have to do with Deacon?"

"As wrong as my actions might have been, my intentions were always the best."

Was there a conspiracy between Deacon and her parents? How often was she going to be reminded that Mercer meant well?

Where Liberty had been quick to soften with her mother, she resisted with her father. The reality was she hadn't known him long or developed strong feelings for him.

Deep down, she wanted to love him. She wanted to say to someone they met, "This is my father," and feel a surge of emotions. Pride. Pleasure. Satisfaction.

"Having good intentions doesn't give you an automatic pass," she said. "You hurt me."

"The only reason Deacon delivered that notice of dissolution to your mother was because I threatened him."

"I know that."

"He told you?"

"I figured as much. You have a track record of using people."

"He requested I hire another attorney. I didn't want to wait that long, so I told him I'd report him to the bar association for taking up with my daughter."

"Oh, my God." She pressed a hand to her chest. "That's a horrible thing to do. Low even for you."

He nodded in agreement, though there was no contrition in his demeanor when he spoke. "Not my most shining moment."

Fury rose inside Liberty. "And you think coming clean with me absolves you of any wrongdoing?"

"Hardly." He chuckled again.

Criminy, the man was infuriating. She could just shake him.

"I am not amused."

He pushed off the stall door. "Don't let Deacon leave. Not without talking to him first."

"You're hardly one to dispense advice."

"I'm right in this case."

"He's made up his mind." Liberty bent and finished wrapping Diablo's last leg. "It won't do any good."

"He'll change his mind if you admit you love him."

Did *everyone* in her family know her feelings for Deacon? What about Ryder? Why not include him, too? She picked up the bottle of liniment and exited the stall, Mercer on her heels.

"I can't just march up to him and say, *Don't leave. I love you.*"

"Why not? That's a dandy idea."

"Because, because…" Her mouth failed to form the words. Annoyed more with herself than Mercer, she headed for the tack room. Of course, he came with her.

"I have a list of regrets a mile long," he said. "Don't you make your own list, too, Libby."

"Libby?"

"It's a nickname."

She'd never had a nickname. Except for honey, which Deacon had called her. To her chagrin, her resolve weakened.

"Talk to him," Mercer said. "If he doesn't listen, then he's not the man you thought he was and certainly not the man for you."

She returned the liniment to the shelf. "You're making your screwup my responsibility to fix. Why don't *you* talk to him?"

"It'd sound better coming from you."

"Forget it."

"Go to his office and take our bucking stock contract." Mercer scratched his bristled jaw as if thinking. "Tell him we need it updated to include the bulls. Before this weekend. That ought to break the ice."

"That is the most pathetic ploy ever. He'll see right through me."

"Great. That'll save you some time."

"I'm not going." She yanked the tack room door shut.

"It's natural to have cold feet. From what your mother says, you don't have a lot of experience at being in love."

"I can't believe I'm standing here listening to this."

"He's a good man, Libby. And I'm pretty sure he loves you, too. Don't let your mother's and my mistakes become yours."

"What am I supposed to do? Drop everything and go hunt him down?"

"Reckless is a small town. He can't be that hard to find."

She hesitated, actually considering going through with it. Something held her back.

"You know what's number one on my list of regrets?" Mercer moved closer to her.

She could hear the lecture before he even started. "Not fighting for Mom when you had the chance."

"Nope. That's number two. My biggest regret is not coming back to Reckless when I first suspected you were my daughter."

A tug pulled at the gaping tear in her heart. "When was that?" she asked in a choked voice.

"When I heard your mom was pregnant again. I'm no genius but even I can do simple math."

"Why didn't you? Come back, I mean."

"I was a drunk. Not a fit father for any child. I'd proved that with your sister. Picking her up at her friend's house and bringing her home when I had no business being behind the wheel."

Liberty blinked. More tears? Seriously, she was crying at the least little thing. Except this wasn't a little thing.

"You were a fit father to Ryder. You stopped drinking when he came to live with you."

"He's not the reason I dried out." Mercer laid a hand on her shoulder. He hadn't touched her since that first day they met in the Flat Iron Restaurant. "It was the stories he told me about his baby sister. I realized what I was missing. What a fool I'd been to abandon my family." He let his hand drop and shrugged. "I stopped drinking."

"But you didn't come back." *For me,* she silently added.

"I did. Several times. Brought Ryder to spend summers here. You were young. Probably don't remember."

She did. The memories were fuzzy but there. She'd

been a bit in awe of the man whom her brother and sister called Dad.

"Your mother." Mercer shrugged again. "She wasn't ready to forgive me, much less let me near you. When I hinted to her that I was your father, she ran me off the place a second time."

"You could have tried harder."

"Yeah. We all could have done things differently." Was he referring to that list of regrets? "I chose to not take any payments for my share of the arena. I thought that the more money your mother had to run the household, the better life she'd be able to give you. My inadequate way of making amends."

"Then why come back now and demand the money?"

"Same as you. I want this family reunited."

"You picked a lousy way of doing it."

"Did I?" The corners of his mouth quirked. "I'm back in Reckless. Your mother and I are working together. And whether she admits it or not, she's starting to take a shine to me."

Liberty couldn't argue that. She'd seen them kissing. One or two of those old sparks were still burning.

"Ryder's coming home," Mercer continued. "I'm spending time with my grandson. And you and I are getting acquainted. That sister of yours." He exhaled slowly. "She's a hard one. I think she'll come around eventually. I'm not going to give up on her."

What an egomaniac, Liberty thought. "Everyone is mad at you for trying to run their lives. How can you say you didn't pick a lousy way? Threats and manipulation?"

"Do you honestly think if I'd been sweet and agreeable and easygoing we'd be working together now?"

"Maybe."

"Maybe?"

"Probably not," she relented.

"Don't throw away your chance at happiness simply because you dislike my methods."

He *had* tried to be a father to her when she was little. Not his fault her mother drove him off. And when she had, he'd done the best he could.

Gosh darn it all. His intentions *were* good. She groaned.

"Okay. I'll talk to Deacon." If she didn't, she'd wonder for the rest of her life what might have been.

"That's my girl. Now, come here."

He didn't wait for her answer, simply pulled her into a bear hug. The scent of his aftershave engulfed her. Liberty closed her eyes and inhaled.

"I'm going to need a copy of our contract," she said when he released her.

"Or you can just tell him about the changes. Seeing as he's here."

"He is?" she squeaked, and looked around.

"That's his truck."

Deacon must have pulled in while she and her mother were talking. Otherwise, she'd have noticed.

"Go on." He gave her a gentle push. "You're wasting daylight."

She stared for a moment, seeing Mercer in a new light. He might not be the picture-perfect father she'd created in her mind all those years growing up, but he was her father, and he did love her.

"Thanks," she said. "For coming home."

"It's going to be okay, Libby."

She nodded. "See you later. Dad."

A wide grin spread across his face. "That you will. Count on it."

DEACON STOOD AT the pens, watching the bulls stomp the ground and bellow noisily. They were a rowdy bunch and seemed to know that practice was starting soon and Walter would be moving them to the bucking chutes. The cowboys riding tonight would get their money's worth.

These pens and those gates were where it all had started. Deacon's journey of the past eleven years. He wasn't usually the melancholy type. Today was an exception.

"Do you have a minute?"

At the feminine voice, Deacon turned. He'd half expected—half hoped—he'd run into Liberty. It was Sunny, however.

"Sure."

She stepped closer. "There's something I want to say to you. An apology I need to issue."

"You talked to Ernie?"

"He came by earlier. Frankly, I was rather startled to learn the accident was intentional and that he'd caused it."

"Because you thought it was me all along?" Deacon wasn't mad anymore. He was curious, though.

"I honestly thought it was an oversight. A mistake. You, or someone, left the gate open." She glanced away momentarily, then back at him. "I should have stood by you more. Defended you. It wouldn't have made a difference in either the arena's reputation or the business. I owed you that much."

"It's all right, Sunny."

"It isn't. You need to know how deeply I regret my actions."

Deacon kept telling himself he was a changed man. Time to prove it.

"Thank you," he said.

She extended her hand. He took it in his, feeling the last of the old wounds heal.

"You're exactly the kind of man I've always hoped Liberty would find.'

"She's exactly the kind of gal I hoped to find."

"Maybe you should tell that to her." Sunny smiled and stepped back.

Liberty stood there, looking prettier than ever. Deacon had seen her talking to Mercer. When had she come over? He was usually more attuned to her, sensing her presence before she appeared.

He hardly noticed Sunny melt away. The next moment she was gone, walking toward Mercer, who waited near the arena. Had the other man heard what Sunny said? Had Liberty?

"Were you going to say goodbye before you left?"

He took a moment to look at her. Just look.

It had been much, much too long since they were this close. Ten days that had felt more like a year. Once he'd let her into his life, she'd become vital to his existence. He understood Mercer's addiction in a way he hadn't before. For Deacon, Liberty was his whiskey.

"I'm not leaving just yet," he said, wondering if she detected the unsteadiness in his voice. "Thought I'd go on a ride. Wanted to see the bulls first."

"Ernie said you were taking a job at that law firm where your friend works."

"They made me a nice offer." Deacon took a step toward her. It didn't lessen the sensation of an insurmountable distance between them.

"Were you going to tell me about it?"

"Yes."

This time, *she* took a step toward *him,* and Deacon felt something he hadn't thought possible. Hope.

"You came back to Reckless to clear your name, and now you have."

"Funny, it doesn't matter anymore."

"What's changed?" She studied him as if searching for signs of the different person he'd become.

"You were right. I needed to prove something to myself more than clear my name."

"Did you?"

"I'm not a coward."

"No, you're not. My family has put you through hell. More than once. And you've stood strong. That takes real courage."

A particularly large bull swung his head and rammed the fence, objecting to Walter's insistence that he follow his mates down the narrow corridor. They were a handful. Sunny's concerns weren't completely unfounded.

"I saw you and Mercer hugging," Deacon said.

"He's trying to be a decent dad."

"That's good."

"But he's still impossible." She sighed indignantly.

"That's part of his charm."

"He told me about threatening to call the bar association and report you. I was shocked."

"Yeah." Deacon pushed back his cowboy hat. "I've yet to find a positive slant to that one."

"I have." She came another step closer. "Not for threatening to call the bar association but him forcing you to deliver the dissolution letter."

"I'm all ears."

"You insisted I needed to repair my relationship with my parents before we could have one. You were right, and that wouldn't have happened without our argument."

"I didn't want to argue."

"I was pretty mad at you for a few days."

"And now?" He took a step toward her.

"Not mad." She shrugged a shoulder.

"What do you really want, Liberty?" There was only

one answer she could give that would keep him from walking away.

"My father suggested I find you. He says our bucking stock contract needs updating to include the bulls."

His disappointment was acute. Like having an arm ripped off.

"I should probably get going. Huck and Confetti need exercising."

She blocked his way. "I told him that was a pathetic ploy, and you'd see right through it."

"Really now."

"Don't leave. Don't take that job in Phoenix. Stay in Reckless. With me."

Deacon grabbed her by the shoulders and hauled her onto her tiptoes so that they were nose to nose. Mouth to mouth.

"How do you feel about me, Liberty? Do you love me? Because I love you, and I've never said that to a woman before."

"Yes, oh, yes!" She threw her arms around his neck. "I love you, Deacon. And I've said it many times. To you. I just didn't let you hear me."

He kissed her then, and in that moment, everything wrong became right. He was holding the woman he loved and she loved him in return.

"Just so you know," he said, when they finally broke apart. "I'm not leaving Reckless."

"You aren't?"

"The job offer's a good one, but I turned down my friend."

"Why?"

"I thought maybe if I stuck around, you'd come to your senses."

"Me!" She swatted him on the chest, then pulled his mouth down for another kiss. A much longer one.

The bulls were gone and in the chutes by the time they started toward the barn, hand in hand.

"You in the mood for company on your ride?" she asked.

He thought of the view from the Aqua Vista Trail and sharing it with Liberty. "Absolutely."

She smiled coyly. "Maybe afterward we can go to your place."

"How 'bout dinner first? At the Flat Iron."

"Dinner out? I was thinking in. Like *in bed*."

He stopped her there in the open area between the barn and arena and cradled her cheek. "I want to go on a date with you, one where we get to know each other. Not talk about business or our families. We can take this slow or fast, however you want. You need to know one thing, though."

"What's that?"

He didn't think he'd ever grow tired of staring into those blue eyes of hers. Especially when they were gazing at him with love and happiness.

"I'm in this for the long haul. I'm not going to propose tonight. But I will. Soon. Ring, down on one knee, the whole nine yards. It's going to happen, honey. If you aren't serious, now's the time to say so."

"I'm serious." She reached up and covered his hand with hers. "I've waited a long time for you, Deacon McCrea. You aren't getting away from me again."

"Glad that's settled."

He'd have kissed her again if not for her parents descending on them.

"Sorry," she muttered under her breath. "They're impossible. They were probably spying on us."

"Then let's give them something worth watching."

Laughing, he swept her up in his arms and twirled them in a circle.

Life with Liberty wasn't going to be boring by any stretch of the imagination, and he couldn't wait to see what the future held. For too long, Reckless had simply been the town where he grew up. By loving him, Liberty had made it his home.

* * * * *

Look for the next book in Cathy McDavid's
RECKLESS, ARIZONA *trilogy*
coming soon!

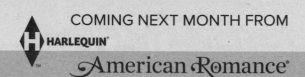
#1509 TRUE BLUE COWBOY
The Cash Brothers
by Marin Thomas

Beth Richards decides to celebrate her divorce by picking up a cowboy, and gorgeous Mack Cash is perfect. After an incredible night, Mack wants to get to know the real Beth—not an easy task when he wakes up alone.

#1510 THE TEXAN'S LITTLE SECRET
Texas Rodeo Barons
by Barbara White Daille

When her dad has an accident, Carly Baron returns home—and faces her former lover Luke Nobel, manager of the Barons' Texas ranch. Their attraction is rekindled, but single dad Luke is certain Carly is hiding something.

#1511 A COWBOY'S HEART
Hitting Rocks Cowboys
by Rebecca Winters

Liz Henson and Connor Bannock have always kept their distance because of their feuding families. Now they're traveling together in close quarters to the National Finals Rodeo...and finally giving in to their forbidden attraction!

#1512 THE COWBOY MEETS HIS MATCH
Fatherhood
by Roxann Delaney

As teenagers, Jake Canfield and Erin Walker fell in love. Now, even though Erin realizes her feelings for Jake have never waned, he's a reminder of the baby she gave up for adoption....

REQUEST YOUR FREE BOOKS!
2 FREE NOVELS PLUS 2 FREE GIFTS!

LOVE, HOME & HAPPINESS

Harlequin American Romance is excited to introduce a
*new six-book continuity—**TEXAS RODEO BARONS!***
Read the following excerpt from
THE TEXAN'S LITTLE SECRET, *where Carly Baron*
confronts her past in the form of cowboy Luke Nobel…

The cowboy standing in the barn doorway started toward the truck. He wore a battered Stetson, the wide brim shading most of his face, but no matter how much she tried to convince herself this was just any old cowhand striding toward her, she couldn't believe the lie.

He halted within arm's reach of her driver's door, his eyes seeming to pin her into her seat. "Carly Baron," he said. "At last."

"Luke." She forced a grin. "Isn't this flattering. Seems like you were just waiting for the chance to run into me."

"I figured it was bound to happen once Brock said you'd come home again. But when I never caught sight of you, I started to wonder if he'd been hitting the pain pills too hard."

"I'm not home again. I'm just visiting."

"The helpful daughter."

"That's me." She shoved open the door and a double dose of attitude made her stand straight in front of him. He stared back without saying a word. Let him look all he wanted. One touch, though, and she'd deck him.

"It's been a long time."

"And you've come a long way." If he picked up on the

added meaning behind her words, he didn't show it. "I hear you're ranch manager now. Daddy's right-hand man. You finally landed the job you'd always wanted."

He got that message, all right. His jaw hardened. "You think that's what it was all about? I wanted to get to your daddy through you?"

"I said that to you then, and you didn't argue. But it looks like you found a way without me, after all."

"Funny. By now, I would have thought you'd grown up some."

"I expected you'd have grown beyond working for my daddy."

"A man's gotta have a job," he said mildly. "And I guess none of us knows what the future has in store."

"I'm not concerned about the future, only in what's happening today. *And* in making sure not to repeat the past."

"Yeah. Well, what's happening in my world today includes managing this ranch. I'd better get back to it."

"That's what Daddy pays you for," she said.

He touched the brim of his Stetson. "See you around."

Not if I can help it.

Look for THE TEXAN'S LITTLE SECRET
by Barbara White Daille, the first installment in the
TEXAS RODEO BARONS *miniseries.*
Available August 2014
wherever books and ebooks are sold.

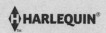
American Romance®

He never expected to see her again!

When Mack Cash's mysterious one-night stand shows up at the dude ranch where he works, he is stunned. And just as he suspected during their night together, Beth Richards is no buckle bunny, despite the getup she was wearing. Instead, she's just the kind of woman he's looking for—sexy, sure, but also down-home and whip-smart.

Mack's obvious attraction is just the boost Beth was looking for after a hurtful divorce. She loves the way he looks at her—and sees her. Except for one thing. He wants a family, and Beth can only disappoint him. She's already failed at love once and she can't go through it again. That's why she has to let Mack go….

Look for
TRUE BLUE COWBOY
by MARIN THOMAS

from *The Cash Brothers* miniseries from
Harlequin American Romance.

Available August 2014 wherever books and ebooks are sold.

Also available now from *The Cash Brothers* miniseries by
Marin Thomas:

THE COWBOY NEXT DOOR
TWINS UNDER THE CHRISTMAS TREE
HER SECRET COWBOY
THE COWBOY'S DESTINY

www.Harlequin.com

HAR75530